John Corey Whaley

WHERE THINGS COME BACK

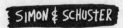

SIMON & SCHUSTER

First published in Great Britain in 2015 by Simon and Schuster UK Ltd
A CBS COMPANY

Originally published in the USA in 2011 by Atheneum Books for Young Readers
an imprint of Simon & Schuster Children's Publishing Division,
1230 Avenue of Americas, New York, BY 10020

1 3 5 7 9 10 8 6 4 2

Simon & Schuster UK Ltd
1st Floor, 222 Gray's Inn Road
London WC1X 8HB

Simon & Schuster Australia, Sydney
Simon & Schuster India, New Delhi

A CIP catalogue record for this book
is available from the British Library.

PB ISBN: 978-1-47112-533-1
Ebook ISBN: 978-1-47112-534-8

This book is a work of fiction. Names, characters, places and
incidents are either the product of the author's imagination or are
usedfictitiously. Any resemblance to actual people living or
dead,events or locales is entirely coincidental.

Printed and bound by CPI Group (UK) Ltd, Croydon, CR0 4YY

www.simonandschuster.co.uk
www.simonandschuster.com.au

FOR *Anita Cooper*,

TEACHER AND FRIEND

Contents

CHAPTER ONE
All the Idealism in the World Couldn't Shake This Feeling

❧ I was seventeen years old when I saw my first dead body. It wasn't my cousin Oslo's. It was a woman who looked to have been around fifty or at least in her late forties. She didn't have any visible bullet holes or scratches, cuts, or bruises, so I assumed that she had just died of some disease or something; her body barely hidden by the thin white sheet as it awaited its placement in the lockers. The second dead body I ever saw *was* my cousin Oslo's. I recognized his dirty brown shoes immediately as the woman wearing the bright white coat grasped the metallic handle and yanked hard to slide the body out from the silvery wall.

"That's him," I said to her.

"You sure?"

"Positive."

His eyes were closed. His lips purple. His arms had bruises and track marks. Nothing was hidden from view, as he had died in a sleeveless white T-shirt, one of the same he had worn nearly every day of his life. There was something white in the corners of his mouth, but I didn't ask what it might be. I didn't really say much after that. The woman waited there for me to cry or say "I'm done," or something. But I didn't do a thing. I just stared at him. And I'm not sure if I was thinking anything at that moment either. I wasn't thinking about missing him or pitying him or even about how angry I was at him. I was just standing there like some ass-hat, mouth half-open and eyes glued to one spot. Eventually the white coat woman broke the silence.

"Do you need any more time?" she asked.

"No thanks. I'm good."

My mother cried on the way home. My little brother, Gabriel, looked anxious, but he kept his headphones on and didn't say much for the duration of our trip. I drove, but I didn't want to because I thought it might rain. I hate driving in the rain. I'd wanted my dad to come along so I wouldn't have to play man for the evening by driving the whole way and making sure everyone ate and all. I didn't so much mind the body identifying. That part was bound to happen, one way or another. Oslo had been shooting shit into his arm since I could remember. He had also frequently been an inconvenience to me. Picking him up at truck stops or crack houses. Telling lies to his mom to cover up his dumb-ass behavior and save him an argument. Loaning him ten dollars here and there and hoping he would buy food with it, but knowing he probably wouldn't. I did it all. We all did. Me. My dad. Even my aunt Julia gave him money so long as he showed up every other day or so, long enough to make her forget that she had failed to raise him right, long enough to make her love him again.

My dad couldn't come because he got a call around five thirty that afternoon to haul some oil well equipment up to Harrison. That's what he does. He hauls things that I don't know anything about and never really care to. All I know is that somebody needs these large pieces of metal that have something to do with pumping oil as soon as possible when they call him. And so he goes at all hours of the day and night. Sometimes he sits at the house for days, reading the paper or novels about dead people (because, apparently, men in their forties are only interested in reading about the lives of presidents, explorers, or criminals). Sometimes we don't see him for two weeks at a time, only hear the sound of him switching trailers in the backyard at three in the morning or leaving messages on the machine to remind Mom to fill a prescription or pay the mortgage.

When we got home from Little Rock, Dad was still gone and the kitchen light was the only thing we could see from the driveway. Gabriel had fallen asleep about twenty minutes before and Mom wasn't far behind him. She leaned over and kissed the side of my head before she got out of the car and walked toward the house. Opening the back door, I kicked at the bottom of Gabriel's shoe. He shot up quick and threw his arms up, as if someone were about to cut his throat. I looked at him the way you look at someone when you're waiting for them to come to their senses—like you're both frustrated with and feeling sorry for them—and then I helped him get his footing. I followed him into the house and Mom was already in his bedroom, already crying again as she talked to a half-asleep Aunt Julia. Soon there was one more crying voice, and Gabriel and I sat up on my bed and listened through the wall as Aunt Julia rambled on and on about wanting to die.

Gabriel was asleep within minutes and the voices in the room next door had nearly gone silent. If they were still talking, they had decided to whisper, perhaps taking into consideration the two teenagers in the next room who had to get up and go to school the next day. Before lying down, I grabbed my leather-bound journal off the nightstand and turned to the first blank page I could find. I jotted down *Oslo After Death*. This would be a great title for a book, I thought. That is what I do sometimes. I jot down titles for books that I one day intend to write. *Oslo After Death* was #71.

I closed the journal, turned off the lamp, and looked at my brother to make sure I hadn't stirred him. He still slept, an impossibly sincere smile on his face. He had a habit of shutting out the world. Habits like this meant that he didn't look up when he walked down the hallway at school. If you look up, then you can avoid being pushed or running into someone or being the convenient target for some ass-hat standing by the water fountain waiting intently for innocent-looking freshmen to walk by with their heads down. My problem was that I wasn't big or tough enough to really protect or defend my little brother in any manner save for my sometimes creative use of sarcasm as distraction. Lucas Cader, though, was quite effective in staving off those common shitheads who liked to pick on Gabriel and his friends. I think, in a way, Lucas felt like it was part of his duty in the world to protect those kids. I'm glad, because it wasn't mine. You see, Lucas had power. He walked down the hall and you noticed him. You noticed his six-two swimmer's build and his messy brown hair that always looked like it was ready for a photo shoot. You noticed how he smiled at the pretty girls but always managed to say something nice or sweet to the not-so-pretty ones. Lucas was the only other guy besides Gabriel that I could stand to be around, simply for the fact that I just didn't like guys all that much. I liked girls and women, but guys really put me off most of the time. Everything is a pissing contest with most guys. With Lucas, I could be my insecure shell of a man and not feel threatened. And Gabriel could walk down the hall and not risk having his backpack thrown into the trash can. And Elizabeth Strawn could feel good about herself for maybe the only time that day she had a huge zit on her cheek.

Being seventeen and bored in a small town, I like to pretend sometimes that I'm a pessimist. *This is the way it is and nothing can sway me from that. Life sucks most of the time. Everything is bullshit. High school sucks. You go to school, work for fifty years, then you die.* Only I can't seem to keep that up for too long before my natural urge to idealize goes into effect. I can't seem to be a pessimist long enough to overlook the possibility of things being overwhelmingly good. But as I lay there in my bed that night with my brother asleep beside me, I couldn't seem to muster up any sort of idealism. The phone call at three that afternoon. The drive to Little Rock. And then the revelation of death. It was all too real. Nothing idealistic about seeing your only cousin ghost white and stone dead. Not much to idealize when you know your aunt is crying herself to sleep next door and nothing can be done.

Like most teenage boys, I, Cullen Witter, was in love with a beautiful girl who had a big, burly boyfriend who would just as soon kick my ass as look at me. His name was Russell Quitman, and I didn't care too much for his brother or parents, either. But I sometimes dislike people by association. The girl's name was Ada Taylor, and she could have probably kicked my ass too. (If you haven't figured it out yet, just about everyone you know could probably kick my ass.) If you lived in Lily, Arkansas, which we all did, then you knew Ada, or at least knew about her. I'm pretty sure even some of the kids in Little Rock and Memphis heard stories about Lily's own black widow.

You see, Ada Taylor had a grim history. As a sophomore in high school, when I was just a freshman, Ada was dating this ass-hat by the name of Conner Bolton. Conner was a senior and made it his personal mission to make every freshman in the school terrified to be caught walking alone or near the bathrooms, lockers, or trash cans. But alas, he died before Christmas break in a car accident. Ada was the only other passenger. She walked away without a scratch. Then, the next year, Ada was dating this okay guy who I used to play G.I. Joes with on the floor of my mom's hair salon. His name was Aaron Lancaster. He didn't even make it to Thanksgiving before he up and drowned in the White River during a thunderstorm. His dad found his empty fishing boat. A search party found his body four days later. I heard it looked like he had been microwaved.

After that, it almost seemed like a ridiculous thing to date Ada Taylor, or even go near her. But that didn't matter much to the young men of Lily, even me. The unspoken philosophy of all those in love with Ada was something like this: If I have to die to get that, then death it is. But there we were with one week of school left and Russell Quitman was still breathing up all the air around him and taking up all the extra table space around him in the lunchroom with his monstrous biceps. I had bet Lucas that Russell wouldn't last past Easter. That cost me ten bucks. You might think it sadistic to bet on an eighteen-year-old boy's death or to talk about it like I wanted it to happen or something. This would just further prove that you'd never met Russell Quitman. Certain people are supposed to be the ones who burn up in fiery crashes or drown in the rapids of a river in the middle of the night. These are the Russell Quitmans of the world.

Dr. Webb says that most people see the world in bubbles. This keeps them comfortable with their place and the places of others. What he means is that most people, in order to feel okay about who they are and where they stand in relation to others, automatically group everyone into stereotypical little bunches. This is why boys who don't like sports or don't have promiscuous sex are always called gay, people who make good grades without studying are always called nerds, and people who seem to have no worries in the world and have a little bit of money are always called preps. As a straight-A student who hated football, I fit into two of these bubbles. This left me with things like Post-it notes saying "Cullen Witter's a fag" stuck to my locker and big black glasses being drawn onto my photo in everyone's yearbooks. Dr. Webb also says that the only way of dealing with the close-minded nature of most southern-born, conservative-leaning people is to either completely ignore their ignorance or to perpetuate it by playing into the set of standards that they subconsciously hold for each particular bubble. In short, if I would have whined about being called a fag, then I would have just been called a fag more often. And if Sara Burch would have ignored the boys in fifth grade when they called her a bookworm, then she might not have become the glorified slut she is today.

There are some, however, who seem to be immune to this epidemic of bubbles. They are people like Gabriel Witter, who is perhaps the most interesting person I've ever known, and I don't say that just because he's my brother. I say it because every morning since he turned eleven or so he would wake up before anyone else in the house, go out onto the porch, and read a chapter of a book. I say it because he listened to bands no one ever heard of. And he had amassed a collection of nearly fifty ties by the time he got into junior high, ties he wore to school every single day. I guess the most interesting thing about Gabriel was that he didn't seem to care at all what people were thinking about him. He walked down the hallway at school with his head down not because he wanted to avoid being seen or dissuade social predators or anything, but simply because he didn't see any reason to lift up his head. It took me a while to get to the point where I would walk both down the middle of the hallway and with my head upright. Of course, walking beside or behind Lucas always made this much easier. Given the choice between looking at Cullen Witter and looking at Lucas Cader, anyone would choose the latter.

I called Russell the Quit Man for two reasons. The first one was obvious, his last name. That's a no-brainer. But the other reason I called him this was much more related to his character. It was because the most frequent thing heard when near Russell Quitman were the cries of whatever prey he was putting into a headlock or holding upside down or tripping in the hallway. "Quit, man. Quit!" How is it that Russell Quitman, the Quit Man, could be so cruel, such a huge douche bag, and still manage to go out with the prettiest girl in town? I call this the Pretty Paradox. Pretty girls always want guys who treat them, and most everyone else, like complete shit. It is perhaps one of the most baffling phenomena in history.

Book Title #72: *Good Things Happening to Bad People.*

I'm not sure why anything like the existence of the Quit Man or girls liking him surprised me in a place like Lily. Living in Lily, Arkansas, is sometimes like living in the land that time forgot. We do have things like Burger King and McDonald's,

9

and we even have a Walmart, but if you are looking for much more than that, you'll just have to keep on driving through. Like most Arkansas towns, Lily does have an abundance of one thing: trees. Lily is all trees and dirt sliced into circles by curved roads. Lily is also water, though. The White River runs right along the edge of town and all the way across the state and over to the Mississippi.

If you've never been to Lily, and I bet you haven't, then you need to know that it is located almost exactly halfway between Little Rock and Memphis. There are 3,947 people, according to the faded green sign on the side of the road as you drive into town, and most of those people are complete ass-hats who tried and subsequently failed to leave this place behind. One unique thing about Lily is that, for a small town in the middle of nowhere, it seems to be a very clean, well-kept sort of place. Lily is the kind of place you'd like to move to some short time before you die. If at any other time in your life you think you need the peace and quiet of Lily, Arkansas, then you should either see a therapist or stay there for a week and try to find anything half-entertaining to do.

Because I have few inner resources, I often found it very difficult to deal with the boredom brought on by living in Lily. My brother never seemed bored, and that only further angered me at the fact that I was most of the time unsettled and unfulfilled in everything I did. Gabriel was happy just reading a book or listening to music or walking around town with Libby Truett, his best friend. Well, I can only sit around listening to music or reading a book for so long before my mind starts to wander and picture images of Ada Taylor diving off Tilman's Dock or flirting with the Quit Man outside of Burke's Burger Box.

On this particular day, two days after my trip to the morgue, I decided to call Lucas and see what he had planned.

"I'm bored to death."

"Wanna go for a drive?" he asked immediately.

"You driving?"

"I'll pick you up in five minutes."

If you had to put Lucas Cader in a bubble, and you might be one of those people who has to do such a thing, then he would fit right smack dab in the middle of the preps. Now, keep in mind that I hate hate hate using stereotypical terms like prep and preppie, but it is unavoidable. These were the words my people, as it were, used to describe those high schoolers who dressed nice, bathed regularly, drove a nice vehicle (or, in Lily, drove a vehicle at all that wasn't their parents'), or were on the football team. Feel free to apply whatever term you yourself would use to refer to this group if you were in my place. Lucas wasn't much like me at all. He played football, for one thing. For another, he had a girlfriend. Her name was Mena Prescott, and she reminded me of the redhead from *The Breakfast Club*. She also made me uncomfortable by always hugging on me or kissing my cheek, always doing something that I assume she thought I would find flattering or sexy, but instead just found annoying and offensive. I also hated her accent. I understand that everyone who lives anywhere can be expected to have an accent, especially those of us down here in the South, but honestly, hearing her voice made me ashamed to be human, much less southern. Here's an example: "Hey, y'all! I went o-ver th-a-y-er la-yast wayeek." Try saying that three times fast.

Lucas pretended to love her as much as she thought he did. But it was all bull, really. As he pulled into my driveway, I let the screen door go with one finger and listened as it *tap-tap-tapped* on the door frame when it shut. The smell of cologne in Lucas's car was overpowering.

"Did you bathe in that shit?" I asked, waving my hand before my face.

"How's your aunt?"

Lucas did this all the time. You would ask him a question, serious or not, and he would manage to skillfully deflect it by bringing up something very important and distracting, out of the blue, and your previous thoughts would be left in the dust, just as my house was as we sped down Eighth Street toward town.

"She's a little better. She's eating now."

"And Gabe?"

"Seems the same to me." I thought about my answer. It seemed wrong in some way.

"You know, he's a good kid," Lucas said.

"I like him all right," I joked.

"I mean, you've got all these kids around here doing bad things. Getting into trouble and getting kicked out of school and all that mess. And then you've got Gabriel. He just sticks out, ya know? Like he's better than this place or something. Know what I'm saying?"

"Yeah," I said. I did not know what he was saying.

"I almost think of him as my little brother sometimes," Lucas said in an oddly serious manner.

"Sell him to you for fifty bucks?"

One could always tell when Lucas was doing that thing where he was lost in his own thoughts, as would often happen when the topic of brothers came up. His eyes would get this certain strength about them, like they were really focusing on what was in front of them. And his lips would purse a little like he was getting ready to whistle. And one could only be left to sit back and witness this spectacle, waiting to see if anything brilliant or cathartic would come about. Usually it all ended within a few minutes, when Lucas would realize that he had gotten himself into an awkward position and made others around him feel uncomfortable. Lucas Cader was not in the habit of making others feel anything but comforted. As soon as we pulled up to Burke's Burger Box, Mena Prescott ran up to his car window, leaned inside, and kissed him on the cheek. Then she walked around to my side, knocked on the window, waited for me to roll it down, and kissed me on the cheek as well. As she climbed into the backseat, I wiped her saliva and lipstick off my face.

"Did you really have to see his body, Cullen?"

She began her questions before Lucas could roll the windows back up and pull out of the parking lot.

"I really did," I said blandly.

Mena Prescott had a past that did not involve innocent, good-natured boys like Lucas. It did, however, involve my overdosed cousin Oslo. Let me sum up their relationship like this: They met at a party when she was a freshman and he was a senior.

They made out, both drunk, and then ran into each other one week later at the grocery store. They dated off and on for several weeks before Mena realized, I presume, that Oslo Fouke was nothing more than a drug addict and a bum. That moment in the car would be the last time Mena Prescott would ever mention Oslo Fouke, at least around me anyway.

When one is sitting in the passenger seat of his best friend's car as an overly enthusiastic hillbilly is ranting in the backseat about being snubbed by a cheerleader at lunch, his mind begins to wander and think about zombies. Here's the thing about zombies: They are supposed to be killed. You just have to do it. Humans are obligated to kill zombies, just as zombies have an obligation to seek out humans and feast on their flesh. It is for this reason that I was imagining Russell Quitman and his friend Neil as zombies, wreaking havoc on Lily and killing men, women, and children. They crept down Main Street, dragging their feet, each having one ankle completely limp and dangling behind him. A woman screamed from a store window. A car sped by and crashed into a nearby tree. The scene was a gruesome one until *I* arrived. Walking slowly and with much confidence, I approached the Quit Man and his minion with a shotgun in one hand and an ax in the other. After idly blowing off Neil's slobbering head, I tossed the shotgun aside and double-gripped the ax. The Quit Man was upon me—his teeth more visible than anything else and his smell causing me to gag. I dug the ax into his leg. He fell to the ground, grasping at my pants as I tried to back away for a good, clean swing at him. I tripped, falling down beside him. Just as his teeth were about to pierce the flesh

14

of my neck, his head was smashed in by a black boot. I looked up to see Lucas Cader, smiling and reaching a hand down. Crowds gathered around us and cheered loudly. The zombies had been defeated. "Lucas! Lucas! Lucas!" The sounds surrounded us as I reestablished my footing and scanned the crowd for my brother. He sat alone on the edge of the sidewalk. He had been crying. Lucas put his hand on my shoulder and whispered into my ear, "He'll be fine. We'll all be fine now."

Book Title #73: *You May Feel a Slight Sting.*

CHAPTER TWO
Mysterious Kids with Shovels

❧   When Benton Sage found out that he would be going on a mission for his church that year, he was overwhelmed with excitement and panic. His stomach felt a sort of queasy rumble as he stood with his sisters and Reverend Hughes, and watched as the entire church circled around them, clasped hands, and began to pray. Ethiopia, he thought, would be the first place he could truly exert his faith. It was his fear of travel, of leaving his comfortable life in Atlanta, of floating mysteriously thirty thousand feet in the air, that made eighteen-year-old Benton feel as if he would collapse onto the church's soft, green carpet as he heard the choir begin to chant amens and hallelujahs behind him.

"Our brother, young Benton Sage, you will surely bring many to the Lord!" Reverend Hughes shouted from the pulpit as the congregation took their seats once again and opened their Bibles.

"I need to know where I can find bread!" Benton Sage said, louder than necessary, to a local in Awasa, Ethiopia, where he had ended up one afternoon after he realized he was in over his head.

"No English."

"English? Anyone?" he shouted, standing among hundreds of people, all picking over fruits and vegetables and swatting away flies as they walked slowly along the narrow, cart-filled street.

"Never mind!" he shouted, holding up one hand until he realized that no one was paying him any attention. He had found bread, or what passed as bread in that area of the world.

After spending a frustrating two and a half minutes trying to figure out how much of what kind of money to give the elderly woman for the bread, Benton Sage walked quickly back to his hotel, which was nothing more than three rooms on the top floor of a small clinic, and up the dimly lit, humid stairwell to his room. Once inside, he devoured nearly the entire loaf and sat on the floor, his back against the bed, crying quietly. It was two days later when Benton was introduced to Rameel, who called him Been-tone Sog. Rameel, who had been converted some five years earlier, had taken it upon himself to contact Benton's church and request help for his ministry, which consisted of traveling across the country to provide food, water, and limited medical attention to small villages with the underlying intention of converting as many people to Christianity as possible.

Rameel kept count of his converts. When Benton Sage arrived to help him, his total was, as he said proudly, 1,740.

"Been-tone Sog, you are going to be the light that my ministry needs!" Rameel said loudly just five minutes into their first conversation.

"I'm glad to be here. I'm ready to help out!" Benton was still talking loudly and slowly, under the impression that he could be understood better if he spoke in this manner.

It was on their first excursion to the west that Benton had a vision of God in a dream. The vision went like this: Benton stood alone on the shore of a vast, menacing ocean. The waves crashed against his bare feet and the wind blew his hair into his eyes. The clouds above the sea became heavy, and just as he began to hear thunder, a wall of dark water poured from the sky and into the sea. He squinted his eyes in the wind and noticed that it was not water, but blood falling from the clouds. Turning to walk away, Benton was stopped by a voice, the voice of God. He turned to see, there amid this chaotic and beautiful downpour, a boy standing on the water with one hand, his left, held up into the air. His mouth did not move, but a slight smile remained there as God's voice introduced the boy to Benton. "This is the angel Gabriel," he said. "Do not fear him." Just before the boy opened his mouth to speak, a large bird flew overhead and landed on the angel's shoulder. It let out a great call just before the angel Gabriel spoke. He then said, with great volume and force, "Benton, you have been called to bring change to the world. You have found favor in God's eyes."

When Benton Sage woke up that next day, in the tent that Rameel had set up for them the night before, just outside of a small village he hadn't learned the name of, he found himself soaked in a cold sweat, his clothes stuck firmly to his skin and his hair flat and dripping. Rameel stood before him, as dark as a shadow and taller than the tent itself. He smiled, but with an expression of remorse or shame. He sent one hand down to Benton and, as he pulled him up from his cot, said, "God has given us a gift this day."

The gift, Benton soon discovered, was a small village called Kwalessa filled with the sick, the dying, and the hungry. They moved from hut to hut, entering each one with smiles and hands full of things like bread and jugs of water and crates of rice and grains.

"Each family will get two loaves of bread, two jugs of water, and one crate. You understand, Been-tone?" he asked, suggesting Benton would try to sway from these directions.

"I understand."

As they exited their fifth hut for the day, Rameel, with a huge smile on his face, nudged Benton in the arm and whispered proudly, "Seventeen-hundred forty-six." Benton smiled back awkwardly, thinking that perhaps Rameel had convinced himself that he could convert tribal peoples to a complex faith like Christianity in as little as twenty minutes. He continued on, though, following Rameel into seven more huts before they returned to their tent and settled in for the night. Rameel, sitting up in his cot, looked pleasantly at his new friend and nodded his head.

"What is it?" Benton asked him.

"You, my friend, are truly a blessing."

"Why do you say that? All I did today was stand beside you and hold jugs of water."

"Because, Been-tone, these heartbroken people are finally listening. It is you, because you are here beside me, because you are a Westerner, because you give them a reason to hope."

When Benton awoke the next morning, he found himself alone in the tent. A single but amazingly bright beam of sunlight had filtered through the tent door and hit him directly in the eyes. He walked out of the tent, which was set up on the curve of a narrow dirt road, and was instantly blinded. Just as his eyes adjusted to the light, Benton heard the voices of several children. He turned around to find that five kids were walking around the curve and past the tent, joking and laughing. He smiled, and squinted to see what they were carrying. They each carried a shovel much like a soldier would carry a rifle, resting on one shoulder and held firmly at the bottom.

"Been-tone!" Rameel shouted, running over to stand before him.

"Good morning."

"You slept well, then?" Rameel asked.

"Very well. Thanks."

"You met the children?" Rameel asked, nodding his head toward the mysterious kids with shovels.

"No. I mean, I just saw them walking by. Where are they going?" Benton was still squinting in the sun.

"They go to dig more graves."

CHAPTER THREE
Take Me to the End of the World

On Tuesdays, Wednesdays, and Saturdays, I worked at a convenience store called Handy Stop, which is located right beside I-40. My job included, but was not limited to, the selling of cigarettes, snacks, sodas, lottery tickets, gasoline, and condoms. Sometimes, when life got shitty, I was forced to clean the restroom, which was around back and required a key from the clerk (me) to gain entry. Those were the moments when I imagined an accidental nuclear test bomb landing right smack-dab on Lily, Arkansas. The mushroom cloud. Can you see its majesty? Can you hear its silent fury? I could, especially when trying to ignore the sweat dripping into my eyes as I thrust a brush into the dark abyss.

Ding-ding. That sound always meant that someone was either entering the store or leaving it.

"Can I help you?" I asked politely as a tall, burly man approached the counter and peered behind me at the wall of cigarettes.

"Gimme a pack a' them Pall Malls."

"Two-fifty."

Ca-ching. Slide. Clank.

"Thanks."

"Thanks."

Ding-ding.

When one is spending twelve hours of his Saturday in a lonely convenience store, his mind begins to wander and think about the way the president can't pronounce "nuclear" and the fact that Lucas's cousin is still in Iraq. He imagines vast oceans of desert sand and how uncomfortable it would be to fight the winds by constantly squinting and keeping one's mouth closed, and also how shitty it would be to discover sand in your ass every time you got undressed. He thinks about his mother clipping an older woman's bangs and asking her about her husband, who is in a nursing home. He imagines his aunt in his little brother's bedroom, crying and alone.

Ding-ding.

The Quit Man cometh, his minion at his heels.

As Russell and Neil browsed around the store, I watched Ada Taylor, sitting all alone in Russell's Jeep, staring at herself in the rearview mirror and having no idea that anyone could see her. She wore a bikini top and I couldn't tell what else for the damn door blocking my view. I liked to imagine that it was a long, wrinkly skirt that danced just above the ground when she walked down the banks of the White River.

"Can I get a pack of Marlboros?" Neil asked coolly.

"No."

"I'm eighteen, dude."

"You're seventeen." His face was going back and forth from normal to zombie (which weren't that different, save for him having no jaw in my imagination).

"Just sell him the cigarettes, queer!" The Quit Man had a way with words.

"Nope."

"Douche," Neil murmured as he tossed a bag of Doritos onto the counter.

Russell walked up to the counter the way I imagine a rapist would and put two bottles of Coke beside the chips. He got out his wallet, pulled out a twenty, and handed it to me. He did not make eye contact.

"Is that it?" I asked.

"That and the gas," he said.

"You didn't get any gas."

With a look of frustration and a loud breath, Russell stormed to the door, opened it (*ding-ding*), and shouted, "Pump the gas, dipshit!"

It was not a long, wrinkly skirt. It was a pair of blue jean shorts that were unbuttoned at the top. When I caught myself staring too much, I turned back to see two full-fledged zombies waiting patiently and arguing about where to drive to next.

"Cullen, what the hell happened to Oslo?" Neil asked out of the blue.

"He died."

"I know he died, man. How did it happen? Did he really OD?"

"We're pretty sure," I answered, peeking over at Ada through the window beside me.

"What a dumb-ass," Russell spurted out.

For a second there was silence. That sort of extreme silence when sounds that you usually don't notice start to quickly become more and more evident and obtrusive, like the buzzing of the freezer in the back of the store and the humming of the air conditioner. Russell and Neil were the first people I had talked to that week who didn't tell me they were sorry for Oslo's death. And oddly enough, I found it kind of nice in that weird "I'd like to forget about real life and pretend that everything is okay" sort of way.

"Fifteen seventy-three."

Ca-ching. Slide. Clank.

"Thanks, guys."

Ding-ding.

Gabriel used to do this thing, when he listened to someone tell a story, where he would rest his elbows on a table, cover his eyes with both hands, and rock back and forth ever so slowly. He was doing this the day after my run-in with the Quit Man, on the countertop in my mother's hair salon as she was telling Penny Giles, the postman's wife, about Aunt Julia and her night terrors. I know this because I was spinning slowly around in the barber's chair to the left of Penny, reading a book about a sixteen-year-old who sucks his thumb.

"She's gonna be fine. Just you wait. It'll take no time at all," Penny Giles said, closing her eyes as a cloud of hairspray enveloped her.

"I hope so, Penny. I really do," my mother said in that work-voice that only Gabriel and I knew was insincere.

"Is she still staying with y'all?"

"Yeah. She's in Gabe's room. The poor boys have been sharing a bed."

"You don't mind, do you, Cullen?" Penny asked, peering at me from the corner of her eye.

I actually didn't mind too much that Gabriel had spent the past four nights in my room. He was relatively quiet, didn't go through my things, and liked to listen to my weird book ideas late at night. When I told him that I wanted to write a book about zombies taking over our town, he suggested that I make myself the hero and said nonchalantly, "You could even have to kill me after I get bitten. Wouldn't that be an awesome twist?" I didn't tell him then, but I had no intention of ever letting him die in any book.

The thing to know about my brother was that even though he was fifteen, he looked to be about the same age as me. Only I'm not sure if that was because he looked older or I looked younger. I like to think it was a healthy mixture of both. The convenient thing about it all was the fact that we were able to share clothes, as long as one of us asked the other nicely. Neither of us was the kind of guy who liked his things tampered with. Gabriel was smart, too, smarter than me even. When we were little, we used to lie up on the roof and Gabriel would point out different constellations. Honestly, I thought he was making most of them up until I looked in an astronomy book at the public library. Which figures, given that I cannot remember one single time that Gabriel ever told anything but the truth. That is not to say, however, that he was rude or outspoken or blunt in any way. If Gabriel was being very quiet, it meant that whatever he wanted to say, which would have been the truth, was inappropriate. That is one way in which we differed greatly. I often found myself in situations where I had, without thinking, said too much to too many with too little caution. This is why Laura Fish still won't talk to me in line at the grocery store.

One such situation occurred that same afternoon just as I was dropping Gabriel off at home. I met my father in the driveway as he was throwing cans of Diet Dr Pepper into his ice chest.

"Cullen, I can't make it to the funeral tomorrow. You'll drive your mother and aunt, right?"

"Sure will. Like always."

Those last two words came out of me before I could manage to stop them. It was too late. My father looked at me as if I was the most ungrateful little shit on the planet. He chucked the last can into his ice chest, slammed the lid down, lit a cigarette, yanked his truck door shut, and drove off.

Here's the thing about my father and me. We got along just fine. Everything had been great between us since he had stopped drinking when I was thirteen. Then one day when I was around sixteen I decided to start being a bastard to him. I had no real explanation for it. Still don't. When I was eleven years old my dad took Gabriel and me to this museum about three hours from Lily. It had big life-size dinosaur skeletons and an aquarium with Arkansas fish and alligators in it. It had a mammoth's fossilized footprint and rock candy in the gift shop. It had a room you could go into that would capture your shadow and a mirror that made you look upside down. And on the way home, as my brother slept in the middle seat between us, my dad told me in a slightly drunken slur that he would, without any hesitation, take me with him to the end of the world. I smiled, confused but happy.

Book Title #74: *Ungrateful Little Shit.*

The next morning, in the churchyard, where I had rarely stood, there seemed to be a familiar feel to the wind brushing lightly against my face and the words being spoken as earnestly as they were eloquently by Reverend Wells.

"We've learned from this that death can hurt us.

Death can surprise us.

It can scare us.

It can keep us up at night.

But we've also learned the things that death cannot do.

It cannot crush our hopes.

It cannot take away the love and support of our friends and family.

It cannot make us lose our unending faith in the world and in God.

Death has saddened us, but it will not prevail."

Dr. Webb says that when someone young dies, it makes older people feel guilty for living. Since Oslo was two years older than me, I felt little guilt in his death. What I felt was disgust and pity. I was sad for my aunt Julia, who could barely utter a sentence without bursting into tears. I was sad for people like Mena Prescott, who tried so hard to pretend that she wasn't affected by it. Mostly, though, I was sad for my brother. He didn't act sad, but I knew him better than that. I knew there were feelings there that weren't being shown. I honestly can't remember one single instance where Gabriel ever interacted with Oslo. Not one time. The only reason *I* had to was because I had a license and because Oslo knew that I was like my dad. I don't say no to people very often.

When one is standing six feet above his cousin's body as his aunt Julia is wailing from her metal folding chair and his mother is whispering, "There, there" in her ear, all he can see is a shiny room full of bodies at the Little Rock City Morgue. He turns around and all he sees is a cemetery full of zombies, half out of their graves. They stumble and drag and scoot over to stand beside him. When one is surrounded by hundreds of zombies and they are all looking down at his only cousin, all he can manage to do is softly sing the words to a song he heard on his little brother's stereo.

And when we are dead,
We all have wings.
We won't need legs to stand.

Reverend Wells teared up toward the end. I saw him casually wipe his left eye with the back of his hand as he ended his prayer and the small crowd began to disperse. Lucas whispered into my ear, "I'll go and get the car." This is the type of person Lucas was—driving the family of the deceased to and from funerals without ever being asked. Gabriel stood beside me. I looked over at him the way you look at someone at a funeral, and he managed one of those I'm-slightly-uncomfortable-and-would-love-to-leave-as-soon-as-possible smiles.

"Is she ever going to stop?" I asked Gabriel, looking in the direction of Aunt Julia.

"Doubt it," he answered.

"You're never going to get your room back."

"You mean you're never going to get *yours* back." He chuckled.

I punched my brother lightly on the right arm the way brothers do to show affection, and we walked over toward the car as Lucas pulled up.

There was a little too much fog around the house for my comfort as we pulled into the driveway and my mother carefully helped Aunt Julia out of the car and into the house.

"Poor Julia," Lucas said, resting his chin on the steering wheel.

"She did the same thing when my grandfather died."

"I was there, Cullen."

"Oh. Never mind."

"Did you hear about that bird?" Lucas asked me, still staring toward the house.

Lucas was one of the smartest and strangest people I knew, and so I wasn't very surprised by his choice of topic.

"What bird?" I asked.

"There's this woodpecker that's been extinct for, like, sixty years. Only, this guy from Oregon or something was down here and he thinks he saw one."

"In Lily?"

"Right outside of town. I think he was canoeing down the river and saw it fly by or something."

"Weird."

"Well, I gotta go. Mom's gonna think I'm out being wild or something," he said, laughing.

When Lucas Cader was twelve years old, he had an older brother who died in a car accident. That was in Little Rock. They moved to Lily at the start of our eighth-grade year. Lucas didn't talk about it very much, but when he did I'm pretty sure I was the only one he talked to. And, in his words, since his mother couldn't stop one child from getting drunk and driving into oncoming traffic on the interstate, he had to suffer the consequences, with daily reports of where he had been, where he was going, and why he was doing both.

This is what I knew about Lucas Cader that most people didn't: He wasn't as happy as he looked. When he wasn't in the hallways at school, he didn't have that toothpaste-commercial smile plastered all over him, and he sure as hell didn't have that hopeful, the-world-is-an-amazing-place-so-let's-get-out-there-and-love-life glimmer in his eyes either. What he had were watery eyes in the bathroom and a look of boredom and confusion when he thought no one was looking. And just before he would go to sleep at night, he would close his eyes tighter than I've ever seen and whisper prayers after crossing his chest. When he was done, he would stare at the ceiling until finally dozing off.

Aunt Julia moved back into her house exactly one week after Oslo was found dead by his friend who used to be a prostitute. Try explaining all that to your fifteen-year-old brother, who still chooses to believe that the world is a good place. That afternoon when Gabriel was collecting some of his things from my room, and I was jotting down some ideas in my notebook, he looked up at me and froze in place.

"What's up?" I asked him uncomfortably, noticing a tear in his right eye.

"What if you die, Cullen?"

"What?"

He sat down on the edge of my bed.

"I mean, what if all of a sudden you up and die and then it's just me here with Mom and Dad and Aunt Julia down the street with her screaming and crying?"

"Gabriel, what makes you think I'm going to die?"

"I don't think you are. I was just thinking about what I'd do if you did, that's all."

"Don't think about stuff like that, okay? You're weirding me out."

When one's slightly shy but sometimes entertaining and dramatic little brother quickly leans in and hugs him tightly, he begins to think about writing a book or making a movie where

31

good guys and bad guys don't shoot each other or fight with swords, but just hug each other to death. His brother begins to cry very softly, and he really seems to have no idea in the world what to do or say or how to get himself out of this situation. He thinks about crying too but knows that he wouldn't be able to make it believable. He finally wraps one arm around his brother and pats his back several times, like he's hugging an old woman at church. His brother finally lets him go.

"Sorry," Gabriel said in a whisper.

"It's fine," I replied, not sure if I believed that or not.

The next day was the last of school before summer break. Why they had it on a Monday I couldn't tell you, but I had no complaints about not having to finish out the week. It was Lucas's and my usual tradition to skip the last day of school, but we had decided to go that day simply because we couldn't think of anything better to do. Also, I wanted to get one last look at Ada Taylor before she graduated and never came back to Lily again. She was one of the few I believed would actually make a life for herself somewhere else; somewhere better.

If you've ever been to school on the very last day of the year, you'll know that the teachers are completely checked out. They usually assign you cleaning duties as soon as you walk in the door and seem nearly pissed off that you even exist that day. It was for this reason that Lucas and I opted to help move desks out of the classrooms for summer cleaning. We would slide a desk to the door, lift it, toss it on top of the last desk we slid out into the hallway, and then start all over. I always found a certain strange comfort in routines like that. And for the rest of that day, when I wasn't moving a desk, my body felt like it should be leaning, grabbing, lifting, and starting over anyway.

Ada Taylor did not show up that day. We knew it was a long shot but were still bummed out to realize that we might never see her again. Lucas put a hand on my shoulder and said, in a strange accent, "Well, brother, it wasn't meant to be. And if it was meant to be, then you've been royally screwed!"

"Could be worse," I said. "I could have slept with her and then died."

"True. Very true, my friend."

"Please stop talking like that."

"Like what?"

"Like a poorly acted James Bond."

"Bastard," he muttered in a perfect Scottish accent.

After school, Lucas, Gabriel, and I went to Mena Prescott's house long enough to walk inside, each get thrown a Coke by her overly enthusiastic father, get briefly interviewed by her nosy mother, and finally get Mena out of there and into the car. We went to this place on the river where Lucas first told me about his brother and where I had, some time after that, experienced an R-rated moment with Laura Fish.

"Where's Libby?" Mena asked, as she realized one member of the group was missing.

"Family vacation," Gabriel answered, a sad look in his eyes.

Lucas and Mena were soon playing around in the water as Gabriel and I were lying on the bank, using our shirts bundled up under our heads for pillows.

"Do you think we'd be famous if we saw one?" Gabriel asked.

"Saw what?" Lucas shouted from the water while being splashed in the face.

"If we were lying out here like this and saw one of those woodpeckers."

"Oh. I dunno if we'd be famous, but I bet we'd at least make the *Lily Press*!" I joked.

"That almost seems pointless," Gabriel added.

"Yep," I agreed.

"I don't see what the big deal is with the bird anyway," Mena shouted while trying to avoid being dunked underwater by Lucas.

"Gabe, you want to take this one?" I said to my brother, having already heard his theory about the woodpecker situation just one night before.

"We need it," he began. "I mean . . . *they* need it," he nodded his head toward town.

"What do you mean?" Lucas asked, he and Mena now listening intently, as we all did when Gabriel decided to share one of his theories.

"Look at our town," Gabriel said, "look at the people. How many happy people do you see in a day? How many people do you see who seem fulfilled?"

"I'm fulfilled," Mena butted in.

"You're young enough to think you can get out of here," Gabriel said without hesitation.

"With me," Lucas added, wrapping one arm around Mena's shoulders.

"Go on, Gabriel," I said, rolling my eyes at the happy couple.

"That's the thing—this is a town full of people who used to be like us. You think anyone in Lily grew up dreaming about raising their families here? You think if they all had a choice, they wouldn't leave tomorrow?"

We got quiet for a few minutes after that. It was one of those moments when you're waiting on someone to say something important or funny or just do *anything* to break you away from the sad thoughts that overwhelm your mind. Thoughts like never having enough money to move away or not getting into college. Thoughts like having to come back to take care of a sick parent and getting stuck here all over again. That's what happened in Lily. People dreamed. People left. And they all came back. It was like Arkansas's version of a black hole; nothing could escape it. I lay there silent beside my brother, my best friend and his girlfriend wading in the water before me, and I knew that we were all just in the prelude to disappointment after disappointment. We joked about Lily all the time but knew full well that we were part of it all. There wasn't anything that set us apart from the manager at the Lily Grocery Store, who just *knew* he'd make it out but never did. We were no different from my parents, both of whom had moved away and moved back to Lily within five years of graduating high school.

So, the fact that Gabriel believed our town needed that bird to exist made absolute sense to me, whether I liked it or not. They needed something to be hopeful about. Nothing in my seventeen-year-old mind was going to change if that damn bird really did show up, because I still had a slight chance of a future. I still had hope in the possibility of starting a life somewhere else. It was easier for me to hate everyone in town than hate myself for being afraid I'd be just like them.

"They need it," Gabriel said, breaking our silence. "They need a reason to believe they're all still here for something."

"So, do you think they'll find it?" Mena asked Gabriel as if he were Yoda or something.

"I think they'll all be disappointed even if they do find it. Nothing's gonna change this place," he said, his tone changing from serious and reflective to that of a seasoned actor's.

"Thanks for the uplifting chat, Gabe," Lucas said, splashing my brother.

"You're welcome!" Gabriel yelled, jumping into the water to attack my friend.

Lucas quickly got him into an immovable headlock and looked in my direction.

"So, no more Quit Man then, huh?" Lucas shouted from the water.

"Hell no!" Gabriel shouted back. We all laughed.

"Well," I said, "that's only until he flunks out of community college and comes right back!"

Book Title #75: *The Black Holes of Arkansas.*

CHAPTER FOUR
The Book of Enoch

After about two weeks of traveling, Benton Sage was starting to get used to the routine of passing out food, water, and Christ as quickly and efficiently as possible. He had talked to his family only once since his departure from Atlanta and just long enough to tell them that he believed he was doing God's work. In doing so, Benton had told his first real lie. He lay awake at night, reading scriptures over and over, racking his brain for some meaning to words he'd been fed and had preached time and time again. Rameel, sitting up in his bed one night, looked over at Benton and said, with sleep in his voice, "You are always with God, Been-tone."

"I'm trying to understand something," Benton said back to him.

"What is it?"

"It's in Hebrews. It says, 'Are they not all ministering spirits sent out to serve for the sake of those who are to inherit salvation?'"

"And?" Rameel sat up farther in his bed.

"I always thought that this was God telling us to go out and save people."

"And you doubt that now?" Rameel asked.

"No. I doubt that I am helping God in any way other than providing food and water. I feel as if we are doing nothing more than reading a few scriptures and then moving on."

"We are, Been-tone. We are giving these people food. And we are giving them water. And, yes, we are trying to *sell* God to them. But, you see, it is not so much in the things we say to them about Christ, but more in the things we do for them that mirror the ways of Christ."

"But how will they know to worship him? How will they know where to look for salvation?" Benton's tone was frustrated.

"They will know that someone is looking after them. And the rest is up to God."

The next day Benton Sage thought constantly about what Rameel had said to him. He watched a small child drink from a jug of water and wet his sun-crusted lips. He heard a mother begin to hum and sing a song and watched as her entire family joined in. He saw children playing with a soccer ball near a field of grain, a field that Rameel had helped to get planted for them. He heard Rameel laughing with a small family inside their hut as he showed them pictures of his church and of his family, telling them stories and singing them songs. Benton Sage sat alone outside a family's hut and wrote a letter home. It read:

> *Dear Reverend Hughes,*
>
> *I am not quite sure that this is the place for me. I feel as if my talents could be of better use somewhere else, somewhere I can speak the language and preach, instead of just stand around and run errands. I understand that God has called me to this place for some reason or another, but either I am not ready to receive that message yet or we have made a mistake. You say, always, to trust in the Lord and he will provide an answer, so I will wait on your response and I will continue to do what is asked of me here, for the Lord, and surely he will hear my cries.*
>
> *Sincerely,*
> *Benton Ezekiel Sage*

Benton was able to mail his letter in Addis Ababa, the capital, and listed Rameel's church as the return address. He was told that a letter to the United States would take somewhere between three and five weeks to reach its destination. He waited patiently and continued his work with Rameel, with whom he became closer as the weeks moved on. He learned that Rameel was married to a British woman named Isadora, and that they had two children together, Ezra, a daughter, and Micah, a son. He learned that Rameel had studied in London, where he learned English, and had met Isadora in a literature class during his last semester.

"It was like looking at the sun and not going blind," Rameel said of his first sight of Isadora.

"That beautiful, huh?" Benton asked.

"Been-tone, my family's faces shine like the light of God."

One morning nearly two months later Rameel walked into the small room where Benton stayed while they were in between travels across the country. The room overlooked a prayer garden that Rameel had designed and built for the church. Benton looked up at Rameel, who seemed worried and was holding an envelope addressed to him. Benton grabbed it from his friend, who slowly walked out of the room, and ripped it open with little hesitation. Inside there was no letter from home. No late card for his birthday the week before. No response from Reverend Hughes. The envelope contained only a single plane ticket.

That night, after Benton had explained that he would be leaving in one week, Rameel looked down at his hands and back up at Benton. He shook his head and began to whisper, though they were the only ones in the dining room.

"Been-tone Sog. You will be missed. I thank the Lord for your time here with me. May he shine his light upon you for all of your days."

It was decided the next day that before Benton left, he would be introduced to Rameel's family, who had been staying in London but would be returning to Addis Ababa for the summer months. Rameel beamed with excitement as they drove up to a white, two-story home with a well-manicured lawn so green that the sun reflecting off it made Benton squint his eyes.

"Isadora's family is very wealthy," Rameel said with humility.

"This is not your home?" Benton asked.

"This home belongs to my wife. I stay here from time to time." Rameel laughed loudly as he parked the car and got out.

Inside, the two children ran and jumped into their father's arms. He picked them both up, held them up over his head, and swooped them back down. They laughed and giggled and their faces lit up. Isadora, a tall, slim, and tan Caucasian woman, approached Benton with one hand extended.

"You must be Benton Sage," she said gracefully.

"Yes. And you must be Isadora?" Benton asked.

"Nice to meet you, Benton. Have you enjoyed your time here?"

"Very much so," Benton said, telling his second real lie.

After Isadora showed Benton the house and introduced him to the children, who thought it funny to keep repeating "BEEN-TONE SOG!" at the top of their lungs, they all sat down for dinner in the formal dining room. Benton tried his best to stomach the food, which had been prepared by a chef, but was put off by the rareness of his steak and the cold soup that was served as an appetizer. During dessert, a chocolate mousse that Benton did enjoy, Isadora began asking him questions about himself, his family, and his life as a missionary.

"Well, this has been my first mission, really. I did do some teaching of the scriptures in New Orleans one summer. Do you know New Orleans?" Benton asked.

"Yes," Isadora replied. "My father calls it the Big Easy. Is this unusual?"

"No. That's what most people call it. I have no idea what it means, though," Benton said, thinking about the nickname.

"And do you have any other hobbies besides helping people, Benton?" Isadora asked.

"You mean like sports, or what?" Benton laughed.

"Like singing or writing. Do you paint or anything like that? My Micah is a beautiful painter and Ezra is learning piano."

"Oh. Well, I've always sort of thought that if the Lord didn't make it, then it doesn't need to be made. So I kind of just stick to the scriptures. Never really considered being an artist or anything. I think it would just distract me," Benton said.

"Well, then, perhaps we should call you Gabriel. Huh, Rameel?" Isadora laughed.

"Yes. Gabriel, the Left Hand of God himself," Rameel joined in, raising his glass of water toward Benton and then taking a sip.

"I don't get it," Benton said, feeling confused and out of place.

"Gabriel, the angel. You know him?" Rameel asked.

"Of course," Benton answered.

"He sent the Grigori to hell," Isadora said.

"The Grigori . . . the fallen angels?" Benton asked, sitting up in his seat.

"Right. But it is said, if you read the Book of Enoch, that he did this because the Grigori were teaching the humans too many things like astrology and the arts," Isadora explained.

"The Book of Enoch?" Benton asked.

"Yes. It is not in your Bible. Only in that one." Rameel pointed to the bookshelf behind him and to a thick, leather-bound edition of the Ethiopian Orthodox Bible.

"They were banished to hell for all eternity because they kept messing with the humans here on Earth. They were nosy and so God, through Gabriel, killed their children and sent them to hell," Isadora explained casually.

"They had children?" Benton asked.

"The Nephilim," Rameel said quietly.

"They were giants. Gabriel killed them all and made their parents watch," Isadora said, and took a sip of water.

CHAPTER FIVE
Love the Bird

꙰ Two weeks into summer break
was how long it took for everyone in town to start talking about
that damn woodpecker. This guy named John Barling started
popping up on the front page of the *Lily Press*, and people in
restaurants and stores began to hassle him for details and even
ask for his autograph. Three weeks into summer break and he
was on *Little Rock Live*, a morning show with two corny hosts
whose hairdos couldn't have been shaken with a sledgehammer.
He talked mostly about himself and how he had decided a
year before that he would come down to Arkansas to find the
"elusive Lazarus woodpecker." When asked why he would do
such a thing as to travel from Oregon to Arkansas to find a bird

that hadn't been seen in sixty years, he said something along the lines of "I knew it wasn't dead all along." Wasn't that convenient? That was like saying, "I knew my keys were here all along" or "I knew you'd win." I knew from the first time I saw John Barling's face that he didn't give a damn about birds, and he sure didn't give a damn about Lily, which he tried his best to compliment in every interview that summer. The other thing I knew about John Barling was that he had been shacked up since February with Shirley Dumas, who lived next door to us with her son, Fulton.

Fulton Dumas, a tall, lanky, and disheveled sixteen-year-old, described John Barling as the most egotistical, maniacal, and power-hungry man he'd ever met. I didn't put too much stock in what Fulton said, given that the only man he had to compare anyone to was his slightly effeminate father. But when I saw John Barling and heard him talking about finding the Lazarus, I knew Fulton had been spot-on. This guy was the ass-hat to end all ass-hats. The last of the great ass-hats. The only man to dethrone the Quit Man to reign as King of the Ass-Hats.

When one is driving his mother's car through town and sees signs taped up in the windows of stores and restaurants that read things like LOVE THE BIRD and LILY: HOME OF THE LAZARUS and SECOND CHANCES HAPPEN IN LILY, he immediately starts to think about what heaven must look and feel like to distract himself from the hellish thoughts that invade his mind. He imagines heaven to be not some huge city with streets of gold and tall, white buildings, but a simple room filled with just enough of the good people to make him smile and feel like the center of attention as he tells a funny joke or talks about a new idea for a book. He sees his brother standing in the corner wearing green flannel pajamas like he did at Christmas five years before, and he sees his mother and father holding hands at the kitchen sink as he caught them doing one time when he was eleven. He sees Lucas Cader tossing a football across the room to his older brother, Alex, who looked just like him, and he hears his aunt Julia singing a hymn that he heard in church when he was eight or so. He sings the chorus out loud, the only part he can remember, as he drives past Burke's Burger Box to see advertised a new product called the Lazarus Burger.

> *Here I am, Lord. Is it I, Lord?*
> *I have heard you calling in the night.*
> *I will go, Lord, if you lead me.*
> *I will hold your people in my heart.*

It's hard to say exactly what bothered me so much about John Barling and the whole bird thing without painting myself as an angry-for-no-real-reason teenager dressed in black and moping around like Charlie Brown all the time. But it was the same for Gabriel, and Lucas, too. It was as if we got the joke that everyone in town had been told. We knew the punch line. And it would've been much easier to sit back while all of Lily fell under the awe-inspiring spell of the possibility of second chances, or rebirth, but we just couldn't do it. I may not have liked the people in Lily that much, but I felt sorry for anyone being massively scammed.

My cynicism had been known, from time to time, to get me into accidental trouble. I was especially cynical in groups, perhaps feeling that a witty cut-down about a stranger would earn me the respect and admiration of friends. This rarely worked. You can only act like a jerk so many times before people stop listening to you. Gabriel broke me of this habit one night after I made fun of a couple leaving a movie theater. "You act like you hate everyone. It must be exhausting." And, having no response, I decided that he was right. My brother, ever innocent, had a way of giving everyone in the world a chance to prove him wrong. First impressions meant nothing to Gabriel. In fact, his dislike for John Barling and his mission stemmed not from cynicism, but from the perspective of an animal rights activist. "If I saw the bird, I wouldn't tell anyone," he said to me one afternoon at home. "People can sort of mess everything up even when they're trying to help."

I had gotten to work at noon, and four hours into my shift I had read an entire book and shown off my expert whistling skills to three junior high school girls who liked to flirt with me while one of their mothers pumped gas outside.

Five hours into my shift brought me to the realization that if I saw the bird, I wouldn't tell anyone either. Not a soul. Like Gabriel said, people only got in the way of things. This is why the bird went away in the first place. How could bringing all those people into its home help it to survive any better? No, the Lazarus would be much better off without John Barling and his little mission of rediscovery.

Just as I was about to resign myself to the fact that I should probably mop the store's dull-brown floor, Lucas Cader came striding through the door (*ding-ding*) with his head bopping from side to side.

"Guess what, my kind clerk of a friend?"

"What?" I asked.

"I have big news."

"Well?" I hated when someone would tell me they had something to tell me instead of just telling me.

"I got you a date!"

"A date?"

"Yes, and I don't mean the fruit." Lucas chuckled.

"Funny. With who?"

"Are you ready for this?" he asked, both his hands pointing at me.

"Yes! Tell me!"

"You may want to sit for this one, Cullen."

"I'm going to kill you and go on a murderous rampage if you don't—"

"Alma Ember," he interrupted with confidence, leaning against the counter and close to my face.

"Alma Ember?"

"That's right. The one, the only. Oh yes, my friend. She's all yours."

"Lucas," I said, "Alma Ember is twenty years old."

"Wrong. She won't be twenty for another month, I'd say."

"Still. I can't date Alma Ember!"

"Why? Is it her name? I know, it's kind of—"

"It's not her name, jackass. I can't date a twenty—"

48

"Nineteen."

"Sorry, a nineteen-year-old girl who wouldn't even talk to me when we sat right beside each other in civics class!"

"Cullen. Cullen, Cullen, Cullen. You were a freshman back then. You were short, awkward, I'm pretty sure you had acne. It's all changed now. She's gone out there into the world. She's seen what places outside Lily have to offer and now she's back, and back for good. That means that she's ready to see what's left in Lily that she hasn't already—"

"Screwed?" I interrupted.

"Experienced," he said, crossing his arms.

"The last thing I heard was she was getting married to some guy in Georgia," I said, confused.

"Yeah, and the divorce is nearly finalized. I made sure of it."

"Lord have mercy. What's wrong with you, Lucas?"

"What's wrong with you, Cullen? That is the question that needs to be answered here. I have arranged a date for you with a beautiful, kind, funny young woman who told me that she couldn't *believe* you didn't have a girlfriend. . . ."

"She said that?"

"Absolutely did. She even mentioned the last time she saw you, how you were so nice and handsome. I swear it."

"You're full of shit."

"No. Just you wait. Tonight."

"Tonight?"

"Yes, tonight at seven o'clock I'll be pulling into your driveway with my woman at my side and yours in the back. Hopefully you'll be waiting there with flowers in hand. What do you say?"

"You've already made the plans?"

"Mena and I are picking her up at six fifty on the dot."

"Fine."

I couldn't help imagining, as I bit into my Lazarus Burger on the way home from work, what it might be like if the bird actually did exist and happened upon one of these sandwiches. The burger itself wasn't made from woodpeckers, of course, but instead was a quarter pound of beef with ketchup, mayonnaise, and barbecue sauce. The red, the white, and the dark brown were supposed to remind one of the bird but only reminded me of ordering the same burger when it was called the Number Three.

"Gabriel," I began as I walked into my brother's room when I got home, "what do you think about the Lazarus Burger?"

"It's just a Number Three without cheese."

"Right. But what about the fact that they are selling a burger that has nothing to do with a bird that probably has nothing to do with this town and isn't even alive anymore?"

"I think you're thinking about a burger too much instead of just eating it." Gabriel turned a page of the book he was reading.

"Think about this." I sat on the edge of his bed. "What if I threw a burger into the woods and the Lazarus, if it existed, flew down and took a bite out of it?"

"Ha! Cannibalism!" Gabriel shouted.

"Ornithological cannibalism! That's even worse!" I shouted back, before jumping into the air and running down the hallway to my room in a childish manner that only brothers exhibit around each other.

At five past seven there was still no one in my driveway except for me, and I didn't have flowers in my hand because Handy Stop didn't sell flowers and neither did Burke's Burger Box. At eleven past seven, Lucas's car could be heard making its way to the end of my gravelly road. Mena had her hand hanging out of her window, letting it fly through the wind, as they pulled up and right beside where I stood. Mena opened the door, hopped out, kissed my cheek, and folded her seat forward to let me in. Once in the backseat, I became quiet and awkward as Lucas looked back and said, "Cullen, you know Alma."

"Hi," I mustered.

"Hi, Cullen. You look great," Alma said.

"So do you, Alma."

"Thanks."

What I noticed about Alma Ember is that she didn't seem nervous at all. I guess that is what the world does to you. Or what growing up does, anyway. She seemed quite comfortable to be riding in the backseat of a seventeen-year-old's car with a bunch of high schoolers who I'm sure she'd told herself she'd never see again. I, on the other hand, couldn't think of a time when I'd been less comfortable. Lucas could tell this from the way my eyes shot at him through the rearview mirror, so he tried his best to distract us all by talking about almost getting bitten by a snake that day while helping Mr. Branch build a fence.

Soon after, we pulled into one of the few functioning drive-in movie theaters in the country and all got out to get some food.

I bought Alma a small popcorn and a Diet Coke and bought the same for myself, feeling a little embarrassed to order a diet drink, but not embarrassed enough to drink a real Coke, which I found and still find to be too syrupy. She kissed me on the cheek to say thank you, and I believe that I felt something quite like the feeling one gets when he drives over a steep hill on a country road. From that small moment forward, I began to grow more and more confident and less and less like the usual me.

I couldn't stay focused on the movie long enough to gain any sort of interest, because Alma Ember had set her popcorn aside and opted instead to nibble on my left earlobe. While that was quite enjoyable, I felt overcome with an uncertainty of what to do with my hands. So I just continued to eat popcorn as Alma Ember continued to cannibalize my left side.

When one suddenly feels a young woman's hand crawling up under his shirt, he instantly pictures her having an argument with her ex-husband, who he imagines is much larger and stronger than he is. He sees himself eating supper with Alma Ember in Pizza Hut when this large man rushes through the door, picks her up with one arm, and smashes his face in with the other. He sees Lucas Cader jumping through the window to pick up a chair and break it across the giant's back. Soon Mena Prescott is on top of the checkout counter doing a cheer that spells L-U-C-A-S and Lucas Cader is holding Cullen Witter's head as red trickles down from his hairline and his eyes go glazy. He dies there, on the dirty, burgundy carpet of Pizza Hut, for a few sessions of mediocre sex with a used-up college dropout who does nails on the weekend for extra cash.

I could have very easily walked Alma Ember into her house that night and walked myself out the next morning, but I didn't. I didn't even leave the car. Alma kissed me on the mouth, backed up, looked let down, and then crawled out of the backseat. Mena Prescott could not stop giggling, and Lucas told Alma to have a nice night.

"That was awkward," Lucas said, driving back across town to my house.

"Very," Mena added.

"What do you mean?" I asked. I knew what they meant.

"I mean, she was ready to take you home, Cullen," Lucas said.

"You think?" I asked. I knew he was right.

"Uhhh. She was all over you all night, you dork," Mena butted in.

"She must be really desperate." I laughed.

"You didn't like her?" Lucas asked.

"She's okay. A little too serious, though."

"Too serious?"

"Yeah. I just wanted to watch a movie and eat some popcorn. That's all."

"Cullen. You're the only guy in the world who would say what you just said, do you know that?"

"Yes, Lucas, I am aware."

"Maybe you just need to date younger girls, you know, ones that aren't so ready to get married and all that shit," Mena suggested.

"Maybe I'm leaving Lily in a year and can probably find someone much better!" I yelled.

"Cullen Witter, folks! He lives in the future, only he does it today!" Lucas shouted out the window as we passed an endless span of trees, grass, and nothingness.

Gabriel wasn't in his room when I got home, so I sat down on his floor and watched an old movie on his TV. Mine had been broken for a week. It took me less than fifteen minutes to fall asleep on his floor. When I woke up I had done that thing where you accidentally roll over on one arm and it goes completely dead in the middle of the night, but since you're asleep you don't know and so it just lies there under you all night and when you eventually wake up, it feels like there's no arm there at all. In the mirror I noticed that the side of my face that had somehow been firmly planted into the wooden floor was solid red and had two creases running horizontally across it. I brushed my teeth. I took a long shower. I washed one side of my face better than the other, thinking that I might wash away the redness. I stepped out of the shower and onto the rug, which rested just beneath the bathroom heater. I lifted my head, closed my eyes, and let the hot air rush across and over my face and down my body, not drying me but warming me enough to regain feeling all over, as if I were riding in a hot air balloon. When I went into the kitchen, my parents were eating breakfast together and talking about bills. I fixed a bowl of Cheerios and sat down beside my dad. He looked over at me and grinned.

"You slept on that floor all night, huh?"

"Yes, I did. And a better night's sleep I can't remember!" I shoveled a spoon full of cereal into my mouth as Dad breathed hard in the place of saying, *Ha! Ha!*

"Where's your brother?" my mom said as she sat down across from me.

"Haven't seen him since yesterday afternoon," I replied.

"Oh, how was your date, Cullen?" Dad asked.

"Boring."

"That's a shame. You'll find the right person one day," Mom added.

Book Title #76: *This Popcorn Tastes Like People.*

It was three hours later and after calling everyone we knew and driving around town twice that we decided to call the police. It was a Thursday when my brother, the Left Hand of God, disappeared. It was on this same Thursday that John Barling appeared on national television to talk about the Lazarus woodpecker and how it had come back from the dead. Lucas Cader had been sitting beside me on the couch all day and into the night, jumping up the same way I did every time the phone rang and shaking or tapping his feet just as I was. Mena Prescott had brought over some food for everyone that evening and had stayed only long enough to reassure me that everything was going to be all right, long enough to tell me that these things happen all the time. I'm not sure why, but I wouldn't talk to anyone but the police for that entire day. Not to my parents. Not to Lucas. I couldn't make myself speak. I wasn't crying. I was just silent, sitting there with my eyes glued to the TV screen, listening to my parents being interviewed by two cops in the dining room. When Lucas crawled onto the floor and fell asleep, I simply let my body fall over onto the now-empty couch and followed his lead, until I was woken up for my turn with the police.

When one has just been questioned by a policeman about the last time he saw his little brother, he walks quickly to the driveway, hops into his mother's green Toyota Corolla, drives five miles to the banks of the White River, and jumps into the water after stripping down to his boxer shorts. Under the water, he screams "FUCK" over and over as water fills his mouth and his nose begins to burn.

Lying faceup on the riverbank with water flowing over my feet and between my toes, I began to imagine that the Lazarus had swooped down and landed beside me on the mud. It approached me very slowly but with the full intention of getting as close as possible. Its beady black eyes and long, white bill kept me from noticing that it stood a good two feet off the ground.

"What do you want?" I asked the bird.

"I want to help you, Cullen Witter," the bird said back, in a voice that sounded quite similar to that of Woody Woodpecker.

"Help me do what?"

"I want to help you find your brother," it said, expanding its huge wings and then tucking them back into its sides.

"You know where he is?" I asked the bird.

"I do. And now I'm going to be famous. I'm going to be the first bird to ever find a missing child. I'm going to be on TV!"

"Cullen!" I heard a shout from above me. It was Lucas.

"Down here!" I yelled back.

"What are you doing?" Lucas asked, looking down at my mostly naked body lying half in the mud and half in the river.

"I needed to cool off."

"Feeling better now?" Lucas asked, maneuvering his way down the rocky little hill that led to the riverbank.

"Not really."

"At least you're talking," he said, sitting down on a big rock that was half-buried in the mud.

"Any news?" I asked.

"Nope," he answered.

"Lucas, he's dead. I know he's dead."

"Cullen, look at me," Lucas said sternly.

I looked up and could barely see him for the sun in my eyes, but noticed the tear streaming all the way down the side of his face, down his neck, and stopping at his shirt collar.

"Your brother is not dead."

"Yes, he is," I said, sitting up.

"Screw you, Cullen," Lucas yelled before punching me in the face and walking back up to his car.

Dr. Webb says that losing a child will oftentimes bring about the end of a marriage. In the two weeks following my brother's vanishing off the face of the Earth, my parents seemed to be closer than ever. My dad had stayed at the house every night, refusing to go on any out-of-town runs or to stay away from my mother for more than a couple of hours at a time. They also became very protective of me around that time, not letting me stay out late or go out of town or even hang out at Lucas's for very long.

I mentioned the punch to Lucas on one such occasion that I was allowed to hang out at his house, and the conversation went a little like this:

"Lucas, you punched me in the face. You maniac."

"I was upset. Sorry."

"It didn't hurt anyway," I said, laughing.

"Cullen, you still have a black eye."

"That's not from you. I slipped and fell on a rock right after you left. It was the damnedest thing!"

"Dork," Lucas said, drawing back his fist and pretending to swing at me again.

Those two weeks were mostly uneventful save for the massive forty-man search party that the police department somehow coaxed into hiking through the woods all around Lily and canoeing down the river. After searching for four days in a row, they had found nothing. In those two weeks, Lucas and I had nearly searched all of the surrounding area ourselves, had kayaked down the river twice, getting out to search random sandbanks and things like that. We found nothing. On the Thursday following Gabriel's disappearance, my family and Lucas all drove to Little Rock, stopping in every small town on the way to post photocopied MISSING posters with my brother's school picture on light poles, park benches, and pay phones, and in the windows of stores. We did the same in Little Rock.

Here's the problem with a fifteen-year-old boy going missing: No one thinks he has been taken. Especially Gabriel, who looked to be my age. Everyone in town, though they didn't say it, was thinking the same thing: Gabriel Witter has finally run away from his family. That, or he went hiking through the woods and either got lost or got eaten by a bear. Here's what I knew: My brother was taken from me. He did not run away, because he wouldn't. He couldn't. He would never. And he'd never gotten lost in his life.

Two weeks to the day after waking up on my brother's bedroom floor, I knocked quickly and nervously on Alma Ember's front door. Her mother opened it, and her eyes were wide and surprised to see me standing at her door at nine in the morning.

"Cullen Witter!"

"Hi, how are you?" I said to her, my hands in my pockets.

"No. How are *you*?"

"Oh. I'm fine."

"Have they found anything yet, baby?" she asked with a hand lightly touching my shoulder.

"No, ma'am. Still nothing."

"Well, I know something's got to turn up sooner or later."

"Yeah."

This is what my life had become in just two short weeks. It now consisted of about a hundred of these same exact conversations a day with everyone I happened to see around town. The monotony of it made me want to disappear too. After a few seconds of silence, Alma's mother finally stepped aside and invited me in. She asked if I was there to see Alma. I said I was. She turned her head slowly, put a hand up beside her mouth, and yelled, "ALMA! CULLEN WITTER IS HERE FOR YOU!" like she was sitting in the stands of a football game.

Alma entered the room, and I suddenly remembered why I had thought to turn down her street and walk up to her door.

"Cullen! Hey!" She hugged my neck. I was getting a lot of hugs around that time.

"Hey. I thought you might wanna do something. I was bored."

"Uhh. Sure. Let me put on some shoes."

When we got into her car (I no longer trusted myself to drive), I looked over at her and she looked very nervous and very quiet.

I said, "Alma, if it's okay with you, can we try not to talk about my brother today? At all?"

"Okay, Cullen."

"Okay?" I asked.

"I understand," she said, and then kissed me on the cheek.

For lack of anything else to talk about, it took only half an hour before Alma Ember and I were lying half in and half out of the White River in the very place that I had talked to an overly confident woodpecker, made out with Laura Fish, and been knocked out cold by my best friend. When I rolled over onto a sharp rock and yelled in pain, Alma Ember mistakenly thought that I was in the vocal throes of passion and continued to flail about on top of me, only pressing my back deeper and deeper into the jagged rock that was nearly at my spine. Finally I had to do the only thing I could think of and powerfully lifted Alma Ember up and back so that she went flying into the water. I stood up, felt my back, and brought forward a hand filled with bright red. Alma began to say things like "You bastard," and "What the hell are you doing?" until she noticed the blood in my hand and I turned around to show her the large, deep cut.

A really awkward phone call home to my parents, a trip to the hospital, seven stitches, and two and a half hours later, I found myself sitting on Alma Ember's bed. I was completely naked save for a pair of gold-toed socks and a cross necklace that I'd found in my brother's room. Alma Ember wore even less than that. After she showed me what being a good wife had taught her—her words, not mine—I fell asleep under the watchful eyes of a dozen or so porcelain dolls.

When one wakes up alone in a partially married woman's childhood bedroom as her mother is vacuuming the carpet and smiling, he thinks about turning into some sort of liquid that could melt right into the bed and seep into the floor and under the house. When he realizes that he is still very naked and covered only by a thin white sheet, he closes his eyes as tightly as possible and prays for God to make a tornado rip through the house and carry the woman away so that he may slip out and make it to his afternoon shift at work. Alma's mother begins to whistle as she vacuums right beside where his face is resting, and then she turns off the vacuum with her foot. She looks down at Cullen Witter as he looks up at her with dread and shame. She leans down, kisses him on the forehead, and continues on with her vacuuming until she exits the room, still whistling the same tune.

"How was it?" Lucas Cader asked me as he hopped up onto the counter at Handy Stop that afternoon.

"Don't be a perv," I said back.

"I can't believe you just went over there like that. Crazy."

"I know. I was bored."

"I wouldn't say bored so much as you were a little bit—"

"Don't say it, Lucas," I said. He said it anyway before hopping down from the counter and grabbing a bag of Doritos.

"We should go to that town meeting tomorrow," he said with a mouth full of chips.

"Why? They haven't even found the damn thing yet."

"Because. It's something going on here. Lily has an event. We *have* to go."

"You can go. I can't be around all those people. Too many 'I'm so sorry' faces."

"Come on. Don't you want to meet the famous John Barling?" Lucas asked sarcastically.

"Oh yeah. I wonder if he'd sign my imaginary autograph book with his imaginary pen from his office where he writes articles about imaginary birds," I joked.

"It *could* be real, don't you think?"

"I think I don't care. I'm tired of seeing posters for that bird in the place of posters for my brother. I'm tired of reading articles about that bird instead of ones about my brother, and I'm tired of hearing John Barling's voice on the radio and seeing his face on the TV when he is talking about that bird instead of talking about my brother."

"Shit," Lucas Cader said quietly.

"Shit, indeed," I replied.

Book Title #77: *Praying for Tornadoes.*

CHAPTER SIX
Benton Sage

෫   Benton Sage found his reception
to be somewhat lukewarm when he returned to Atlanta that
humid June morning. His father leaned against a wall, arms
crossed and eyes glaring at the floor as if to indicate that he did
not wish to be spoken to. His mother hugged his neck in a way
that suggested he needed a hug very badly. And his sisters, the
twins, kissed each of his cheeks before saying, "Welcome home,
brother," and walking toward the escalator.

Benton would learn later that day that Reverend Hughes
wished to see him as soon as possible. Benton assumed that he had
already been given another, better mission to serve his church.
In Reverend Hughes's large office, the sun filtering through

the stained glass heated up the room to a sweat-inducing temperature. Benton wiped his forehead clean as Reverend Hughes began to speak.

"Benton," he said, "you are a bright boy."

"Thank you, sir."

"You're what, nineteen?"

"Eighteen, sir. I graduated early," Benton said proudly.

"Ah, yes. I seem to remember that. Anyway, what I was saying was that you are such a bright young boy that I think we might need to reconsider your duties for this church."

"I'm sorry?" Benton asked.

"I believe we have perhaps chosen you too quickly to be a missionary. What I thought was great potential to spread the word of God turned out to be, well . . ."

"Reverend," Benton interrupted, "I want to do this. I want to go out there and change people. It just wasn't possible where you sent me. That's not the way it worked."

"I know the way it works, Benton. I've been on nearly fifteen missions myself. I've been all over the world. I know how these things go."

"Then you know that Rameel's ministry consists of more talk about rice and grain than about Jesus?" Benton was beginning to get flustered.

"I know that Rameel was chosen by God to help all those people."

"But he's not helping them. He's just prolonging their lives. They are still damned when he leaves them. They are fed, but still damned!" Benton began to raise his voice.

64

"Benton, you have somehow lost sight of your mission as a Christian. I'm sorry, but we will not be sending you anywhere else."

Benton Sage had, since he was a young boy, one ultimate goal in mind at all times: to make his father proud of him. He also learned as a young boy that doing this required a strict and sometimes exhausting devotion to religion. At eight, Benton had learned to impress his father by reading scripture at the dinner table. This, as it turns out, often saved him from the beatings received by his two sisters. At nine, he learned to remember scriptures by singing them in his head. At ten, he was asked to recite a scripture during an Easter Sunday church service. When he messed up on two words, his father glared at him from his seat. Benton thought of running away that afternoon, of never going home to be punished. But he couldn't do it. He couldn't leave his siblings and his mother behind to bear the brunt of "Reverend Rambo," as he and his sisters jokingly called him.

"Benton," his father said that Easter night, sitting on the edge of his bed.

"Yes?"

"You disappointed your mother and me today, son," he said in a somber voice.

"I know, and I'm sorry. I really tried," he defended himself.

"Don't make up excuses. It isn't worth it. You said you knew the scripture and you didn't. Tomorrow, when your sisters are out playing, you'll be up here reading that scripture over and over until you know it."

"But I do know it. I just got nervous," Benton began to whine.

65

"You got nervous because you were ashamed of yourself. As well you should have been. I was ashamed of you and so was God," he said as he walked out of the room, switching off the light.

Benton Sage, bathed in complete darkness, whimpered and cried like an injured animal left for dead. He repeated the scripture aloud for no one to hear. He repeated it again. And again. He did this until sleep finally took him, and as soon as he woke up the next morning, he began to recite the scripture once more. He said it while brushing his teeth, his speech muffled by the toothbrush and toothpaste. He said it in the shower, water shooting into his mouth with every word. He spoke it to himself on the school bus, causing three different kids to move farther away from him for fear he had lost his mind.

At sixteen, Benton asked a girl named Susie to the Homecoming dance at his school. That night, as he adjusted his tie in the bathroom mirror and made his way to the door, he was stopped by his father. He ordered Benton to sit down.

"I have bad news," his father said.

"What? What happened? Is everyone all right?"

"Yes. Everyone's fine. It's your date. It isn't going to work out," said his father, sitting down across from his son.

"What? What are you talking about? I'm on my way to pick her up now."

"No, you aren't. I just got off the phone with her mother, who was quite displeased to hear what I had to tell her about little Susie." He shook his head.

"What did you have to tell her?" Benton asked.

"Well, it turns out that, and I have this on good authority, little Susie was seen kissing and hanging all over that pathetic and sinful kid of Stanley Baker's."

"Chip? Chip Baker? Yeah, they used to go out. Not anymore." Benton looked down at the floor. He knew what was coming and wondered why he was even slightly surprised.

"So you thought it was okay to go gallivanting around with some little harlot? I really thought better of you, Benton. Oh well. It's no matter now. Date's off. You can take off that tie."

With that, his father left the room, and Benton, anger boiling up from places he hadn't known existed, clenched his fists tightly and, for a few moments, forgot how to breathe. He wanted to get up, walk out, and pick up Susie at her house; continue with the plans he'd been excited about for weeks. But he couldn't. His father wouldn't have it. He couldn't disappoint him. He couldn't be with some skanky girl like that. He was better than that. He knew better. And as he wiped a tear out of the corner of his eye, he stood up, pulled at the tie around his neck, and headed back to his bedroom. The next morning, at breakfast, Benton sat across from his father with the hope that the date wouldn't be brought up; he wanted the entire thing to just fade away. Just as he went to sip his orange juice, his father, never looking up from his plate of food, said slowly, "I'm proud of you, son, for trusting that I know what's best." Few times in his life had Benton felt that good. He couldn't explain it, not even to himself, but just those few words from his dad made all the anger and worry seem worth it.

But at eighteen, Benton had failed to live up to his father's standards once again. He had traveled halfway around the world, slept in dirt-floor huts, given food and water to the poor and dying, but still hadn't impressed Mr. Jackson Sage. Upon his return home and after hearing of his conversation with Reverend Hughes, Benton's father chose to stop acknowledging his son altogether. As if this wasn't bad enough, Benton was nearly shunned by his entire family, who, save for the occasional "How are you?" or "Could you pass the salt?" seemed oblivious to his very existence. They wanted the same thing he wanted: to know they were doing something that pleased their father. Nothing else in the world seemed to matter above that. He watched his father discuss school with his sisters and cooking with his mother. He watched them all gather in the dining room for Bible study and laugh through television shows in the living room. He wasn't angry with his mother and sisters, because he'd have done the same thing. He would have sacrificed any one of them to know that what he was doing was making his father happy. He had worked for years to earn another moment like that one at the breakfast table—that moment when his father was proud of him. But he had failed. Feeling as if he could take no more, Benton began making phone calls to each university to which he had applied the previous year, before he went to Ethiopia and before he let his father down for the last time. Surely, he thought, one of his scholarship offers was still good. He could just go away one day.

CHAPTER SEVEN
Neighbors

❧   My aunt Julia had been in piss-poor shape since Gabriel left, only adding to the stress and worry of my mother, whom I sat watching one afternoon in the third week of our search. In an attempt to take advantage of our town's recent foray into national fame and to distract herself from the thought that my brother was lying dead in a barn somewhere, she had introduced the Woodpecker haircut. It was for young boys, mostly, and consisted of a Mohawk-style cut with the tips of the standing hair died a bright red, in honor of John Barling's imaginary friend. I thought it was ridiculous but couldn't help watching her every time she completely destroyed a kid's head with her clippers and dye. Duke Lister was the first one to get the haircut, and as soon as all the other twelve-year-old boys in town saw him posing for pictures in front of the huge wooden cutout of the Lazarus, which had replaced an old dogtrot cabin as the main attraction of the city park, they all filled my mom's salon with ten-dollar bills in hand.

"Have you ever seen such a thing, Cullen?" my mom asked me as she massacred Caleb Cooper's seven-year-old head of hair.

"Sure haven't."

At what point my mother decided it was appropriate to pretend to be okay, I had no real clue. What I assumed was that she was trying her best to go about life in as normal a way as she had three weeks earlier in the hopes that Gabriel would reappear just as easily as he had vanished. My father, on the other hand, stayed on the phone pretty much all day long. He talked to sheriff's departments all over the state. He contacted newspapers to print missing ads, but few would agree to publishing articles about a possible runaway. His plan was to make sure that Gabriel's picture was in every newspaper in the state. He was also working on setting up a website, with the help of the kid who fixed computers at Wilson's Furniture Store.

It is hard to explain why, after only three weeks, I had lost all hope that my brother would be found. It did go in phases, though. One day I would wake up thinking, *This is it. He's coming home today*, and the next day it would be more like, *They're going to find his body today.* The only way I could comfort myself was to imagine that my brother had, in fact, just gotten fed up with us and run away. I pictured him in New York City, getting a job as a mail boy in a big company and working his way up to a management position after going to night classes. I saw him in a coffee shop asking a girl to marry him and becoming a father soon thereafter. I saw him looking at a framed pictured of him and me and replacing it with one of his new family. I saw him smiling. He was endlessly smiling.

I was getting tired of my parents hugging me every night. I was getting tired of Lucas Cader sleeping on my floor. I was tired of Aunt Julia's crying every single day, whether I saw it in person or heard it through the phone. Mostly, though, I was getting sick and damn tired of hearing and reading and seeing shit about that damn woodpecker. And sitting up one night in my bed as Lucas flipped through channels on my TV, I wrote this sentence down in my book, the same one I keep my titles in: *If I had a gun, I would shoot the Lazarus woodpecker in the face.*

Fulton Dumas gave me the creeps. It wasn't only because I'd caught him giving me the odd stare-down on more than one occasion, but also because of the way he would say a sentence and then repeat it back to himself under his breath. He also gave Lucas Cader the creeps, so much so that Lucas had developed a theory that Fulton should be investigated in my brother's disappearance.

"They questioned him and his mom the same way they did us, Lucas."

"It doesn't matter. People who do things like that know how to hide the truth. I don't trust him." Lucas stared through my bedroom window at the Dumases' house next door.

"I think you're just getting paranoid. Why would he be so stupid? Who takes someone from the house next door?"

"Exactly. It's the perfect plan: kidnap the next-door neighbor. No one would ever be so dumb as to put themselves so close to the crime scene. And no one would ever suspect the neighbor, either. That's why he did it. He's sitting over there right now, doing God knows what." Lucas shivered.

"You've got to calm down."

"No. I can't. Let's go over there."

"What? No."

"Yes. Come on."

Lucas Cader stormed down my hallway and out the front door. His long, serious stride let me know quickly that he had the full intention of going into Fulton's house. I ran after him.

"Lucas, this is ridiculous."

"No. I have to do this."

He rang the doorbell.

Ding-dong.

He rang the doorbell again.

Ding-dong.

And again without pause.

Ding-dong.

The door opened slowly, the way it would in a horror movie. Shirley Dumas stood before us.

"Can I help you boys?"

"Have you seen Gabriel Witter, ma'am?" Lucas asked without any hesitation.

"No. Is he back?"

"No. Is he here?" Lucas was not letting up.

"What are you talking about, boy?" she asked, confused.

"Is your son here, ma'am?" Lucas asked, stepping into the house and walking past her. I stood on the porch, eyes and mouth wide open.

"Yes, can I *help* you, Lucas?" She was beginning to get agitated. I stayed on the porch.

"Fulton!" Lucas shouted, and began to walk down the hallway to Fulton's bedroom.

"Well, go on with him, I guess," Shirley said, waving me past.

In Fulton's room I became fully aware of why I had never dared to set foot into that house before. His bed was covered by a G.I. Joe blanket, and on top of it sat what had to have been some forty or fifty stuffed animals. The walls couldn't be seen for the many posters that had been tacked and taped and glued up. The posters were of things like kittens and monkeys and bears. Fulton was sitting at his computer with a pair of headphones on. He was singing an eighties song out loud when we entered.

"FULTON!" Lucas shouted, tapping him on the shoulder.

He turned around quickly and took off the headphones. He looked up at Lucas and over at me. He looked at Lucas again, and then back at me. He did this two more times before Lucas began.

"Fulton Dumas, do you know where Gabriel Witter is?"

"No," he said, his expression changing suddenly from surprised embarrassment to sadness.

"Are you sure?" Lucas asked.

"Why would I know where he is?"

"I don't know, Fulton. Why do you need a thousand stuffed bears? Have you seen Gabriel Witter?"

"NO!" Fulton stood up. He was getting angry now as Lucas continued his interrogation. I didn't try to stop him because I couldn't think of anything to say. Also, after seeing the room, I figured I'd give Lucas a chance to prove me wrong. I couldn't watch, though, so I turned around and pretended to admire one of Fulton's many posters.

"Were you in love with Gabriel Witter?"

"Lucas, come on," I had to interrupt, still too uncomfortable to watch.

"Shut up, Cullen. Were you, Fulton?"

"NO!"

Suddenly the room was quiet, and someone was grabbing my shoulders from behind. It was Fulton. He turned me around and looked me dead in the eyes.

"Cullen," he began, "I am so, so sorry that your brother is gone. He was a good one. Very nice and very forgiving and very much like you." With that said, and then whispered back under his breath, he wrapped his arms around me and hugged me tightly. I looked at Lucas, whose anger had turned to remorse as he witnessed Fulton Dumas beginning to cry with his head buried into my shoulder blade.

"It's okay, Fulton," Lucas said.

"Yeah. Everything's fine. He'll turn up," I added.

"I was just messin' around, really," Lucas said.

Fulton let go and walked out of the room. We walked down

the hall and out of the house in silence. In the front yard I looked over at Lucas, and he was chewing on his bottom lip. He was doing that look that he did when he was overthinking something.

"It wasn't Fulton. I was wrong," he said.

"You think?" I joked.

"It was John Barling," he said confidently as he walked into my house.

The Lazarus woodpecker was last seen in a forest in North Louisiana known as the Singer Tract. Despite pleas from the National Audubon Society and a collection of southern governors, the Chicago Mill and Lumber Company, which held sole logging rights to the area, clear-cut the forest in 1944. It was then that the last known Lazarus woodpecker, a female nicknamed Gertrude, was officially not-to-be-found. The Lazarus was the world's largest woodpecker, beating out the imperial woodpecker by just one inch in length. John Barling claimed to have had a gut feeling that if he left his job at the University of Oregon and moved to Lily, Arkansas, he would be able to rediscover the Lazarus and prove that it was never extinct at all. In doing so, he left behind two children, a wife who had no college degree or work experience, and a mortgage. These are the things that Fulton Dumas had discovered about him. One day, some months after he had moved to Lily and bedded Fulton's mom, John Barling went canoeing for the umpteenth time down a small stretch of the White River that flows right on the edge of town. On his canoe trip that afternoon, John Barling claimed that he saw a Lazarus woodpecker fly quickly over his head and land on a huge oak tree. He quietly took out a camera but hesitated, knowing that the sound would scare the bird away. He opted instead to record the bird as it knocked its long bill repeatedly into the tree. He then got just what he needed: The bird let out a loud call that, according to the National Ornithological Institute, is unique to that particular species. So, with just a small digital recording in hand, John Barling contacted the NOI, and soon my hometown was filled with people who had devoted their lives to the study and viewing of birds.

On the fourth week after my brother had gone missing, there was still no sign of him to be found. During that same week, there was still not one single picture of that damn woodpecker. Yet my town was overrun with more people than it could manage. Every bed-and-breakfast was full for the first time in nearly a decade, and the Lily Motel changed its name to the Lazarus Motel, which made me angry as I passed it one particular afternoon on my way to work.

Aside from tourists and birdwatchers, all of whom I refused to talk to, most of the people who came into the store that day were truck drivers who needed to stock up on energy drinks and use the bathroom for longer than I felt was necessary for any human. As I was spraying the bathroom key down with Lysol, a tall man walked in (*ding-ding*) wearing khaki from head to toe. It was John Barling, the damn bird guy. He walked around the store, whistling, hands in pockets, stupid safari-style hat on his fat head, and I wondered what it would be like to sit in a college class with him as the professor. He picked up a candy bar. He put it back down. He picked it up again, read the back, and put it down again. He did the same thing with about three other candy bars until he finally just grabbed a random one from the shelf, walked up, and set it on the counter.

"What's my damage?" he asked in a sad I-desperately-wish-I-could-pull-off-this-southern-charm-thing kind of way.

"Eighty-seven cents," I said without energy.

"Aren't you my neighbor?" he asked.

"I don't think so." I did not want to talk to John Barling anymore.

"Yeah, you are. Hey, did they ever find your brother?"

"No. Haven't seen him around by any chance, have you?" I asked almost as seriously as I was sarcastic.

"Can't say that I have. What a shame. Maybe he'll turn up soon. I hope so anyway."

"I hope that bird turns up soon too," I said, not able to help myself.

John Barling didn't say anything else as he walked out the door (*ding-ding*) with a puzzled look on his face.

Book Title #78: *It Is Not a Sin to Kill a Woodpecker.*

CHAPTER EIGHT
The Tower Above the Earth

𝔢   That August, as Benton stepped into his dormitory at the University of Atlanta, he breathed deeply, closed his eyes, and fell backward onto his new bed. He then heard the flushing of a toilet from the bathroom and, as the door swung open, sat up to see who was there. Before him stood a tall, lean, and muscular boy around his age with neatly combed brown hair, piercing eyes, and a serious look about him.

"You Benton Sage?" the boy said.

"Yeah," Benton said, standing up and extending his hand. "Nice to meet you."

"Cabot Searcy. Nice to meet you, too, Benton," he said, his serious look melting away.

"You been here long?" Benton asked.

"Just long enough to get lost a few times," he joked, dropping down onto his bed.

The two laughed and talked for a while before deciding to walk around the hall to meet some of their new neighbors. Within ten minutes they had met a French major named Lucy, a journalism student named Thomas, and two sorority girls with undeclared majors. Back in their room, the two began unpacking and, before long, found themselves settled in and ready for bed.

"Busy day tomorrow," Cabot said from his bed, the room completely dark.

"Yeah. I hear this orientation thing lasts forever," Benton added.

"Hey, you never told me what you're gonna do with your English degree," Cabot said.

"Oh. I'm gonna be a writer," Benton said for the first time ever.

"Cool. I'm studying philosophy 'cause, well, I'm gonna change the world."

Benton Sage found college to be less interesting than high school only because the girls there seemed even ditzier and more drunken and the guys all seemed a bit too preoccupied with their own bodies, always lifting weights or talking about lifting weights or secretly staring down at their own biceps in the middle of a history lecture.

"I've got no need for muscles," Benton told Cabot Searcy one day at lunch.

"Why's that?"

"Because writers never have to beat anyone up or lift anything heavy. At least I don't think they do," he joked.

"I guess you're right. Just don't piss anyone off with any of your books," Cabot said, laughing.

Cabot Searcy had the kind of confidence that made it difficult for whoever was around him to pay anyone else any attention at all. When Cabot Searcy began to speak, the entire room centered on him. When he laughed, the entire room began to laugh. When he seemed angry, the entire room scowled and frowned. And girls, well, they practically lined up outside of Cabot and Benton's room, waiting their turns to be touched by greatness. Benton, on the other hand, had yet to ask even one girl out and spent much of his time in the school library or coffee shop, always reading. One particular night, as Cabot Searcy was coming in late from a date, he looked over at Benton, who was reading some thick novel, and began to talk. Benton, of course, immediately listened.

"You don't like girls," Cabot said in a serious manner.

"What?" Benton asked.

"If you're gay, it's fine. My cousin's gay. Doesn't bother me."

"I'm not gay," Benton said, sitting up in bed.

"No, really. It's fine. Just fess up already."

"Cabot, shut up."

"Fine. All right. So why do you sit in this room every night reading instead of coming out and having fun?"

"I just never feel like going anywhere. I just wanna sit here and study."

"It's got to get old," Cabot said, shaking his head, almost sounding truly concerned.

"It doesn't. Maybe you should study more yourself," Benton said, turning out his bedside lamp and lying back down.

It was not Benton Sage who was bothered by the conversation that night. Cabot Searcy, staring at the ceiling and struggling to fall asleep, could not help but think about how many times he had fallen asleep in class that semester or how many people he had hired to write research papers for him. He couldn't help but remember the two classes he had already dropped out of or the midterm in geology that he'd flunked. And so, in an English class the next day, Cabot Searcy sat straight up in his seat, his eyes glued to the chalkboard, his ears tuned to the lecture, his finger scanning the book for details. He highlighted every important line. He bookmarked every referenced page. He scribbled notes in the margins. Cabot Searcy began to care about learning not for the sake of making good grades, but because he still wanted to change the world.

"I passed. Can you believe that?" Cabot asked Benton on the last day of the semester.

"Really?" Benton asked.

"Yeah. My parents are gonna flip. All that studying pay off?"

"No. I have to retake two classes," Benton answered.

"Oh," Cabot said, for lack of anything else to say.

While most everyone else was home visiting family for Christmas break, Benton Sage opted to stay behind and begin work on what would be his first novel. Cabot Searcy, gathering his things, told Benton that he was welcome to come to Vidalia with him for the week, but Benton said he could use the quiet time to work on some things and get his head straight. Benton Sage, having written only one page in four days, celebrated Christmas morning by watching a rerun of *The Wonder Years* and eating a candy bar. When he called home to talk to his mother, no one answered. When he thought of how his sisters always sang "O Holy Night" on Christmas Eve, he teared up. Benton Sage no longer believed in Christmas, because he felt that God had misled him. He had tried to help the world, but the world wouldn't let him. That night, just as the church bells began to ring midnight at the First Baptist on Washington Street, Benton was walking up the stairwell of the bell tower. When the twelfth bell had rung, Benton felt air rush against his face, his arms outstretched on both sides. He heard the quiet singing of Christmas carols. His lungs breathed in one final cold breath as his body became part of the earth.

CHAPTER NINE
In Defense of Irrationality

❧ "I just don't like that guy," I said to Lucas about John Barling, one afternoon five weeks after Gabriel played Casper.

"Then we'll just have to kill him," Lucas replied confidently, with one eyebrow raised.

It took me a few seconds of staring into Lucas's eyes to verify that he was joking. Around that time he had begun to say and do things that, as Dr. Webb says, were signs of some sort of nervous breakdown or stress-induced mania. He refused to sleep anywhere other than my bedroom floor, he started driving me to work and staying with me during my entire shift, and he began researching suspected kidnappings across the state via his laptop computer.

"This kid was missing for three years and his uncle had him the whole time!" Lucas yelled to me one morning while I was brushing my teeth.

"So?" I said back, dripping toothpaste onto the counter.

"So, do you have any crazy uncles?"

"No!" I laughed, although I knew Lucas Cader was dead serious.

When one enters his kitchen to find his mother, father, and best friend all seated in front of a stack of uneaten pancakes, he knows that something strange has happened. He instantly remembers the last time his entire family sat there together and can just faintly hear the sound of his brother impersonating their father's laugh, which was known to be surprisingly high-pitched and awkward. He sees his father turn red, trying his best to hold in his laughter as Gabriel stands up and begins to dance as he had witnessed their mother doing while dusting a few days before. Samuel Witter then loses it, tears stream down his face. Sarah Witter follows, holding her stomach tightly as she bends over in embarrassment and hilarity. Cullen Witter sits at the end of the table, eyes watering, smile hurting, and watches his brother in awe.

As I sat down in between Lucas Cader and my father, I caught a glimpse of the headline on the front of the newspaper that hid his face from view. It read LILY EMBRACES NATIONAL CELEBRITY. I knew instantly that what followed was another article about everyone in town being so damn obsessed with that bird. I knew that someone had been interviewed about all the visitors in town from all over the country and that they'd said things

84

like "I can't believe it!" and "Have you ever seen such a thing in your whole life?" Feeling vomit rise up in my throat, I turned to Lucas to see that he had his eyes closed and his hands clasped together. I looked across the table at my mother, who had a tear falling down her cheek, and asked her, in a whisper, what was wrong.

"That boy Russell Quitman had a car wreck in Florida and broke his neck," she said softly. "Isn't that terrible?"

It took a minute to get the image of the Quit Man lying bloody on the pavement out of my head.

"Is he okay?" I asked.

"He's paralyzed," Lucas said, his eyes still closed, "from the waist down."

"Good God. That's awful," I said, surprised that I actually meant it.

"My mom called a few minutes ago and said his mother had called and told her," Lucas added. "She said he'd be in the hospital down there for another few weeks."

"Oh." I didn't know what to say.

"Poor Janette," my mother added, referring to Russell's mom.

"Poor Don. He's got to pay the doctor bills," my dad said from behind the paper.

"Poor Ada," I said finally. "This makes three for three."

"No," Lucas interrupted, "they broke up two weeks ago. I didn't tell you?"

"Uh, no."

"They did. She told him she wanted to be single when she went to college." Lucas laughed, but then stopped himself quickly.

"Just think," I said, "if they'd still been together, he'd probably be dead."

"Probably," Lucas agreed.

Alma Ember was beginning to become less of a welcome distraction and more of an inconvenience to me. A seventeen-year-old boy cannot be expected to adequately replace a nineteen-year-old woman's college-educated husband. And so, with the utmost maturity and respect, I told Alma Ember, in her parents' shag-carpeted living room, that we probably shouldn't see each other anymore. When she started to cry, I felt very nervous and was racking my brain for some sort of reaction, some wise word, some supportive, comforting gesture. I came up with nothing. Gabriel Witter would have been able to have her laughing by the time he left the room. I saw her still crying through the window as I backed out of the driveway.

Only once before then had I made a girl cry. This was, of course, Laura Fish. After just three dates, the two of us, sixteen years old at the time, decided to get more acquainted one sunny afternoon at the previously mentioned spot on the bank of the White River. Once our clothes were back on and we were back in Laura's car, I began to laugh. She asked why. I refused to tell her. She stopped the car and pulled over onto the side of the road. She asked why again. I refused, shaking my head, my hand clasped over my mouth. She began to cry.

"What the hell?" I asked.

"Why are you laughing at me?"

"I'm not. I mean, I just got tickled, I guess. It's nothing," I said the way I do when I think the person I'm talking to is being irrational.

"You're a jerk," she said back.

"Laura, I'm not laughing at you. I'm laughing at the fact that we just went through all of that to lay beside each other naked in the mud for an hour and then go home," I said.

"Get out," she said calmly, unlocking the doors.

"Laura, I didn't *do* anything!"

"I'm sorry I'm not the whore you're looking for, Cullen. Now get out."

"Laura," I said, standing outside her car with the door open, "I was laughing at us, not at you. I'm not looking for a whore. I don't even like whores. I've never even met a whore!"

"Well, good luck. Jerk!"

She sped off, the door slamming shut soon after as I was left coughing in the cloud of dust thrown up by her tires. Walking down the dirt road that day, I imagined myself being brave and hitchhiking the three miles to my house. I then imagined a one-toothed truck driver picking me up and asking me about my friends and hobbies. This made me queasy. And just as I began to smile thinking about Laura Fish running naked into the river, a truck came speeding up beside me and stopped. Again, I coughed in the dust. Just as I could see in front of me again, Joe Eddie Fish, Laura's fifteen-year-old brother, who'd been driving illegally since he was thirteen, was walking toward me.

"My sister says you're a creep," he said loudly.

"Your sister is crazy," I said back, not being able to stop myself.

"You wanna say that again?" he asked.

"Can we just talk for a minute?" I said, trying not to laugh at the absurdity of my situation.

"Talk is cheap," he said back.

"Really, Joe Eddie? Are you comfortable with what you just said?"

"Shut up, Cullen. Damn. I'm trying to be intimidatin'!" he whined.

"Joe Eddie, you used to run through the sprinkler in my front yard. It's hard to be scared of you," I said, laughing.

"Shit, Cullen. I'm s'posed to be kickin' your ass." He laughed too.

"Were you really gonna do it, Joe Eddie?" I asked.

"I thought I was."

"Will you just drive me home instead?"

"Come on."

I told Joe Eddie the entire story as he drove me home, and he laughed right along with me. He talked about how his sister overreacted to just about everything anyone said to her and about how his mother did the same thing. I told Joe Eddie that it was a shame that he and Gabriel didn't hang out anymore, and he said that Gabriel was too smart for him. "He makes me feel stupid. But it isn't his fault. We aren't on the same level, ya know?" I felt like that was one of the first adult conversations Joe Eddie had ever had. I also felt like he wasn't as dumb as everyone made him feel.

"Thanks for the ride," I said, unbuckling my seat belt.

"Cullen," he said, "I'm sorry."

"For what?"

Just as soon as the words had left my lips, Joe Eddie's fist met my right eye. Black. For a few seconds I saw black. Then, as the stinging intensified and I rolled myself out of the truck, my head began to throb and I hobbled toward the house. Joe Eddie Fish had, in his eyes, defended his sister's honor. He had done this even though he believed her to be crazy. For that, I was not angry at Joe Eddie. He had principles. That's more than I could say for most. The next day Laura Fish passed me in the hallway with a smirk. My eye was purple. Lucas laughed and nudged my arm. Gabriel whistled the theme to *Rocky*.

Now that Russell Quitman's fate had been sealed, I was feeling very guilty for all the zombie fantasies in which I had chopped off his head. That being said, I was feeling less and less guilty for all the nonzombie fantasies I had about Ada Taylor and her wrinkly skirt. I was having one such fantasy while shelving cigarettes one Saturday morning in July. My fantasy was soon interrupted when someone entered the store. *Ding-ding.*

"Hello," I said, never taking my eyes from the wall of cigarettes.

"You should get a haircut," a voice said from behind me. It was a girl's voice; that's all I knew in that moment.

"Why do I need . . . ," I began as I turned around to see Ada Taylor standing before me, a green wooden counter and a thick awkwardness between us.

"Because it's gettin' too long. You tryin' to look like a surfer or somethin'?" she joked.

"No." I had no idea what to say to her as she nonchalantly carried on a conversation with me.

"You're acting weird, Cullen Witter," she said with a grin.

"Oh, I just didn't expect to see you, that's all," I said shakily.

"Well, I came in here to see you. If that's okay." She suddenly seemed anxious.

"It's fine, Ada. How've you been?" I mustered up the courage to try and ignore the fact that a beautiful girl whom I'd never said more than hi to had come to visit me at work.

"I'm here because I heard about your brother a long time ago and I haven't gotten the chance to see you since." Her tone had gone from playful to serious.

"Oh. It's fine. You didn't have to—"

"I did," she interrupted. "I've been thinking about it for weeks, since I heard, and I've felt so guilty for not helping y'all look for him. I'm ashamed that I didn't do anything but think about you, instead of calling to check on you or coming to see you."

"Ada," I said, "we barely know each other. It's fine." I used my talking-to-an-irrational-person voice again.

"I know we aren't friends and I know this is stupid, but I can't stop thinking about this. I just got to town and this is the first place I came."

Her eyes had more sincerity in them than I'd seen in just about anyone who had given me an "I'm so sorry" or "We're praying for your family" in the past few weeks. This beautiful, talented, intelligent girl had really been worried about me and about my family and my brother. She had *really* cared. And in that moment, I suddenly felt unable to stand up any longer. I backed up slowly to the metal chair behind me and eased down. I closed my eyes. My hands were shaking.

"Cullen?" she whispered. "Are you all right?"

I didn't answer her because when I tried to speak, I felt as if I'd either throw up or scream, and I didn't want to do either in front of Ada Taylor. I lowered my head down onto my knees, and as my body began to shake uncontrollably, I felt a warm arm wrap around my shoulders. Ada Taylor knelt beside me on the floor as I cried for the first time over the thought that my favorite person in the world was probably dead.

Book Title #79: *The Business of Making Girls Cry*.

Chapter Ten
Cabot Searcy

▬   It is said, in the Book of Enoch, that two hundred angels led by Azazel, the keeper of God's throne, came to Earth after falling in love with the human women they had watched. And in doing so, these fallen angels began to reproduce with the daughters of Earth and bore what were then called the Nephilim, great giants who consumed all the possessions of man and, because man could not stop them, eventually began devouring him as well. And after destroying the birds, beasts, reptiles, and fish of the Earth, the Nephilim began to eat one another's flesh and drink one another's blood.

At the same time, the fallen angels, known then as the Grigori (or Watchers), began teaching all the remaining humans the arts of war, astrology, and vanity. It was then that the heavens heard the cries of those men who had died from the lawlessness of the Earth. And God ordered his left hand, the angel Gabriel, to go down to Earth and stop the lawlessness. And so Gabriel, along with the angels Michael, Uriel, and Raphael, caused the Nephilim to wage war against one another. Their fathers, the Grigori, were then bound to hell for all eternity for the sins they had brought to Earth.

Then God spoke to Noah, the great-grandson of Enoch, instructing him to save his family and the animals from the great flood that would cleanse the Earth of the corrupted humans. And Enoch, who did not die but was taken away by God and made into the angel Metatron, kept God's throne, invented the art of writing, and communicated God's word to those on Earth.

When Cabot Searcy was told that his roommate and friend had killed himself, he immediately walked into the bathroom of his parents' house, splashed warm water onto his face, and stared at his reflection as tears began to roll down his cheeks. Benton, he thought, wouldn't do such a thing as jump off a bell tower on Christmas Day. But he had, and now Cabot Searcy would face his second semester of college alone and without his friend. After drying his face, he straightened his eyelids and shoulders and walked out of the bathroom, where he was then tackled by his little sister Megan, who growled like a lion and pretended to claw at his chest.

It should not have been his responsibility to do it, but Cabot

Searcy had waited two long weeks for Benton Sage's family to send for his things and no one had, so he began to box up the half of the room that did not belong to him. By doing so, Cabot Searcy felt that he would be able to keep himself from getting too distracted by Benton's death and move on with his life. On the second day of slowly rifling through Benton's things, Cabot Searcy came upon a photo album labeled with a strip of masking tape and a black marker. It read: FAMILY.

The album was like any other, complete with a few childhood photos of playing in the yard and by the pool and things like that. There were several shots of a teenage Benton sitting by his siblings on the couch or making a silly face at the camera while doing homework. One showed Benton hanging upside down from a swing set as his mother sat nearby, her face blandly gazing toward him. And only one photo showed his father, dressed in a suit and tie, shoulders broad and powerful, with a neatly trimmed mustache. Benton stood next to him, a small space between their arms, and what looked to be uncomfortable smiles on each of their faces. On the last page in the album, there was a picture of Benton standing next to a very tall, very slim black man, whose smile seemed to leave little room for Benton's, who squinted, smirking slightly as the man held his shoulder tightly.

Three boxes were more than enough to hold all of Benton's things, and so Cabot Searcy began the final task of taking off the sheets and bedspread from Benton's bed, planning to take it all downstairs for someone to hopefully mail home to Benton's parents. However, it was when he ripped the bottom sheet off that Cabot found what looked like a diary of some sort stuffed under the mattress. The book was narrow, bound by a cardboardlike cover, and had a rubber band wrapped around it. Cabot set it down on the floor next to the bed and continued to fold the sheets, stacking them neatly into the last box. He sat on his bed, staring down at the book. He picked up the book. He set the book on the bed next to him. He picked it up again, and then put it back down. He carried the first box, filled mostly with books and CDs, down to the first floor. When he walked back into his room, Cabot Searcy went straight for the book. He quickly tore off the rubber band and turned to page one. It read, in bold black ink:

> *Warning: The following pages, whether used as a*
> *journal or for ideas, are most assuredly filled with*
> *melancholy, cynicism, and woe.*

Cabot grinned as he flipped through the pages of the book to find often short, mostly random musings over things ranging from strange phrases Benton had heard to television shows he'd watched to people he had encountered. Benton's first entry in the book was dated about three months before he began college, so Cabot quickly thumbed through to find the point at which he had met Benton. The page numbered forty-seven in the top corner began like this:

> *I met my new roommate today. He seems nice enough,*
> *although I wouldn't ever want to make him angry.*

> *I think he seems to like me, which is good. He was*
> *already flirting with the girls next door.*

Cabot Searcy laughed. He closed the book and lugged the second box down the hall and down the three flights of stairs to the main floor. Before picking up the third box, Cabot tossed the little book on top of the sheets and began his journey downstairs one last time. Just outside the office where he'd left the first two boxes, Cabot set the box down, snatched the book from the top, shoved it in his back pocket, and then left the box downstairs, as he had done twice before. Back in his room, he put the book in the drawer of his nightstand and went to bed.

In 1773, a Scottish explorer named James Bruce heard wind that a surviving copy of the Book of Enoch existed in Ethiopia. There, Bruce discovered three copies of the ancient text and returned to Europe with them, leading to their later translation into English by Oxford professor Dr. Richard Laurence. At that time, the books had been missing for nearly one thousand years, having been banned from the church by powerful theologians who claimed the text heretical and ordered all copies to be burned or shredded. Later, copies of the book were found among the Dead Sea Scrolls, dating them back to a time before Jesus Christ, who himself is said to have referenced it through his ideas and elaborations on the fall and judgment of man. Though many Christian and Jewish theologians give little to no credit to the book, which at one time was considered an accompanying apocryphal, or secret writing, to the New Testament, there is one church that includes it within its Christian Bible, this being the Ethiopian Orthodox Church. This church adheres to many of the strict practices also promoted by Orthodox Judaism and has somewhere around forty million followers, such as Rameel and Isadora Desta of Addis Ababa.

It took only two nights of casually flipping through the book for Cabot Searcy to read all of Benton Sage's mostly comical entries. He had laughed loudly when he read Benton's description of him as "looking much smarter than he actually is." The book was not even half full, and though he hesitated for a moment, Cabot Searcy decided to write something on the first blank page he saw. He dug around at the bottom of his book bag until he finally came up with a pen, and after taking the cap off with his teeth, he began to write.

> *Benton Sage died when he leapt from a bell tower on Christmas Day. He will be sorely missed.*

With that done, Cabot Searcy decided that it was time to perhaps find something else to do with the book, simply because the thought of keeping something once owned by a dead person gave him a very uneasy feeling, which would explain the two nights in a row he was unable to sleep. And just as he was about to rewrap the rubber band around the book, Cabot used his thumb to quickly fan through the book's pages, causing a noise that he remembered coming from an elderly man in church years before. He did it again, though, because he thought he had seen something on one of the pages near the back. He stopped the fanning and turned a few pages, and there he saw written in black ink:

> *And heal the earth which the angels have corrupted, and*
> *proclaim the healing of the earth, that they may heal the*
> *plague, and that all the children of men may not perish*
> *through all the secret things that the Watchers have*
> *disclosed and have taught their sons. And the whole*
> *earth has been corrupted through the works that were*
> *taught by Azazel: to him ascribe all sin.*
> —*The Book of Enoch 10:7–8*

Chapter Eleven
Vilonia Kline

❧　　　　　Because my father refusing to
go back to work had nearly exhausted our funds, my family
decided to accept donations set up through the local bank by the
First United Methodist Church of Lily, which we attended on
a semiyearly basis. The website my dad had set up proved only
to serve as a forum for a few ass-hats to send in false sightings
of my brother and a few housewives from surrounding states
to write in and express their "deepest regrets" and shit like
that. Lucas's research had done little more than make him the
most paranoid person I'd ever met, and my mother had finally
accepted the fact that people would eventually stop getting bad
haircuts just because they felt sorry for her.

I, on the other hand, found some strange sort of refuge in being with Ada Taylor, whom I quickly discovered was a lot more than just a pretty girl in unbuttoned blue jean shorts and a bikini top.

"Maybe he just woke up and said, 'Screw it,' and hopped on a train to, I dunno, New Mexico or something," Ada suggested, running her fingers lightly through my hair, my head in her lap.

"He wouldn't do that," I replied.

"Or maybe," she continued, "he was a spy for the government all along and he's being held captive in Russia or something. Maybe your brother is the most dangerous man on the planet!" She laughed.

"Maybe," I said.

"Do you hope he's run away, Cullen?" she asked, her tone still almost lighthearted.

"What I hope is that the sky opened up and he floated right up into it."

"Me too, then," she said, leaning down to kiss my forehead.

At some point over that next week I had decided that even if Ada Taylor was showing me attention and affection purely because she felt sorry for me, I was still madly in love with her. Lucas told me that she would eventually be the end of me, and when I reminded him that I had little to live for anyway, he didn't speak to me for two whole days. When he did return to my house, however, he did so with Mena Prescott by his side and a smirk on his face.

"I'm sorry, Cullen. I was mad," he said, looking down at the floor.

"It's fine, Lucas. You're allowed to get mad every now and then," I said.

"Aww, you two should kiss and make it official!" Mena shouted, crossing her arms and tilting her head to one side.

"Well, not with you here, Mena," Lucas joked.

"Yeah, we save that for when you fall asleep at the movies," I said, winking.

"Okay, that's enough. You're creeping me out," Mena said.

Mena Prescott had become, at some point over that summer, someone I learned to truly appreciate, which is not something I do easily with most people. For at least one night a week since Gabriel's disappearance, Mena had shown up at our house with a sack full of groceries and cooked an entire meal, dessert and all. She had also begun helping my mother around the salon, refusing payment, and had hassled the editor of the *Lily Press* to run Gabriel's photo on the front page until he was found. How she accomplished that last one we were all too hesitant to ask and too appreciative to care either way. And the more I began to appreciate what she did for my family, the less her accent and hyperactivity bothered me. And regardless of whether or not he really loved her, Lucas seemed to be spending more and more time with Mena and less time sitting on the counter of the store as I shelved cigarettes and mopped the floor.

The road was lonely and desolate and all those things that a road is not supposed to be when you are driving down it at five minutes to midnight after leaving your new girlfriend's house and wondering whether or not she really exists or is part of your imagination—some mental coping mechanism that has taken over your thoughts and actions. I began to think about my brother and how, when he was in a car at nighttime, he would always roll down the window and rest his head on the door, staring up into the sky and whistling or humming some song he was obsessed with. My brother was often obsessed with songs. He obsessed over books the same way, which was evident when you looked in his back pocket, on any given day, to find a fingerprint-stained copy of *The Catcher in the Rye*, which I had read out loud to him when he was twelve years old. The week before he left, Gabriel claimed to have read it for the eleventh time.

When I got home I went into Gabriel's room to search for the book. It was in his top dresser drawer, next to his empty wallet and a magazine about bands and musicians that I'd never heard of but knew that Gabriel would have been an expert on. There was a folded piece of paper marking the last page he'd read in the book, and as I opened it, the bookmark fell to the floor. I picked it up and began to unfold it, not even pretending to be hesitant about being nosy. On it was scribbled handwriting that could barely be deciphered, which was something else my brother and I had in common, and it read:

> *You came to take us. All things go, all things go. To recreate us. All things grow, all things grow. We had our mindset. All things know, all things know. You had to find it. All things go, all things go.*

When my brother could find nothing better to do, he would jot down the lyrics to whatever song was playing in his head. It was usually something I'd never heard before. In this particular case, it was a song about a man driving with his friend to Chicago and sleeping in parking lots. One time, about a year and a half before that, I had found a notebook with pages and pages of songs, all of which had played in my brother's head. He never sang them, just wrote them down diligently as if he had been assigned to or something. Similarly, whenever I used to think a conversation I'd had with someone was especially funny or enlightening, I would jot it down in my notebook, the same one I kept my book titles in. An example of one such conversation was the one I had with Officer Lansing of the Lily Police Department on the day after my brother went missing. It went something like this:

"You say you saw your brother yesterday afternoon, right?"

"Yes. He was sitting in his room," I answered robotically.

"What did you two talk about?"

"Birds."

"Birds?" Officer Lansing asked quickly.

"Well, actually, we were talking about hamburgers."

"Hamburgers? Not birds, then?"

"We were talking about the Lazarus Burger and how it was just a Number Three without cheese." I laughed.

"It isn't very good, is it?" Officer Lansing joked, breaking away from his serious demeanor.

"It's just a Number Three," I said, shaking my head.

Dr. Webb says that sometimes the sibling of a missing child

goes through some sort of strange angry episode. This happens when the child who is not missing begins to feel embittered toward the child who is missing purely because he or she is getting all the attention of everyone around. This is one of those strange concepts like Munchausen's syndrome, where you make yourself sick to get people to notice you. I will tell you this: I did not crave attention from anyone. Actually, I found the amount of attention that I was getting to be very off-putting. My least favorite thing about that summer was the way in which strangers looked at me in stores, restaurants, and places like that. I would walk by them or enter a room and suddenly, as if they had practiced and been waiting to do so, people would lean their heads down or turn to someone next to them and begin to whisper, saying things, I assumed, like, "That's the boy's brother," and "They still haven't found that poor brother of his," and "He seems to be holding up all right, but I hear his mother's going crazy."

It was not my mother who was going crazy that summer. It was my father. After the website he'd spent a fortune to get running had failed to do anything but waste his time, he began to read book after book on missing children. My mother, on the other hand, pretended that everything was okay. Maybe she was going crazy too, but it was a less offensive and in-your-face crazy, so it was a bit easier to swallow.

It was the day after my brother had been gone for six weeks that my father brought Vilonia Kline into our house and sat her down in the living room. My mother, Lucas Cader, Mena Prescott, and I all stood across from her on the other side of the room. My father, awkwardly enough, introduced her as "someone who I think can help us find Gabriel."

"What?" my mother asked.

"Sarah, Ms. Kline is a spiritual guide," my father began.

"Oh please," my mother butted in.

"Mom," I whispered, nudging her arm.

"Ms. Kline has agreed to help us, so let's all be supportive of her while she asks us a few things, okay?" My dad's voice remained calm and steadfast.

"Fine," my mother said.

"Sure," I said.

Lucas Cader and Mena Prescott said nothing but looked over at me with expressions that suggested that they were either about to laugh or run for the door. They did neither.

"First, I need a shirt of Gabriel's. Something he wore often, like a favorite T-shirt or something," Ms. Kline said in a saner manner than I expected.

My father handed her Gabriel's favorite T-shirt, a black one with PINK FLOYD written across the chest.

"Okay, did Gabriel have a favorite hobby or sport, something like that?" she asked, managing to look up at all of us at once.

"He read books a lot," Lucas said uncomfortably, looking over at my mother for a silent approval of his participation.

"Yeah, and he listened to a lot of music," my father added.

"Well. Let me see." Ms. Kline closed her eyes and thought for a minute. "Bring me whatever book may have been his favorite, or perhaps the last book he had read, and we'll start from there, okay?"

Vilonia Kline, who my father said had helped solve four other missing persons cases, held my brother's T-shirt, his copy of *The Catcher in the Rye*, and his previous year's school picture in her hands. She closed her eyes. We all looked at one another with eyebrows raised, standing uncomfortably in our places, swaying back and forth. I was biting my lips and letting each one of my fingers meet my thumbs over and over again.

"He was a smart boy." Ms. Kline broke our painful silence.

"He was," my dad agreed.

"And he was funny, too, wasn't he?"

"Definitely," Lucas said.

"Where is the last place any of you saw him?"

"His room," I said.

"Can I see it?" she asked, standing up, his things still in her hands.

She sat on the edge of Gabriel's bed, her right hand lightly touching his pillow, her fingers wriggling like worms. We stood in the hallway, my parents half in and half out of the room. She lay down on the bed and put her head on the place where my brother's had been the last time I'd seen him. We all sort of inched forward slowly when she did this, but then settled back to our places and watched. Her eyes closed, she began to hum. I'm pretty sure it was a very slowed-down version of "Stairway to Heaven." I looked over at Lucas. He was angry. Mena held his hand and twirled her hair nervously. My mother stared at my father with a look of disgust and pity. Vilonia Kline broke the silence once again, standing up to do so.

"He was religious, wasn't he?" she asked loudly.

"Why do you say that?" my mother asked.

"There have been many prayers spoken here."

A single tear fell quickly down the side of my father's face. My mother stood closer to him and put a hand on his shoulder. Lucas Cader's forehead rested lightly on the back of my shoulder before I heard him sniffle and walk quickly down the hallway and outside. Mena followed him. I stood in place. I looked into Vilonia Kline's light green eyes and stepped closer.

"Can you find him?" I asked softly.

"He is not near water," she said plainly.

"Is that it? That's all you've got?" I stepped even closer.

"He has left a lot of energy here. He had a strong spirit."

I remember hearing nothing as I walked down the hallway. It was as if the ringing in my ears was so loud that noise became silence. The door swung open, hitting the outside wall, and I stomped down the front steps. Lucas and Mena sat at the bottom, both staring at the ground. I walked past them. I grabbed the sides of my head with my hands, pulling my hair back. I brought my hands back to cover my eyes and mouth.

"What is it, Cullen?" Lucas asked quietly.

I said nothing.

"Cullen, why don't you sit down?" Mena suggested.

I did not sit down.

"Cullen!" Lucas stood up, grabbing both my arms and lightly shaking me.

"She said he HAD a strong spirit!" I yelled, tears now running into my mouth.

"What?" Lucas asked, still holding my arms.

107

"She said he *had* a strong spirit," I cried. "She said *had*."

I lowered my body down to the ground and Lucas, not letting go, lowered his with mine. We sat on the grass. Mena stood looking down at us.

"What does she know, Cullen?" Lucas whispered. "She doesn't know. She doesn't."

"But what if she does?" I asked.

"She doesn't."

He looked at me with a half smile. I wiped my eyes with my shirt collar and stood up. I sat down on the bottom step leading up to the porch, and Lucas and Mena sat beside me. I started laughing. I still tasted tears in my mouth, still felt snot running from my nose.

"What's funny?" Mena asked.

"There's a psychic in my house and I'm crying on the porch."

"And?" Lucas said.

"And I'm wondering how much more absurd this can all get."

"Well," Lucas began, "a couple of guys said they saw the Lazarus yesterday. Said it swooped down in front of their truck, right behind a diesel, over on Highway Nineteen. That absurd enough for you?"

"Yeah. At least I'm not seeing imaginary birds like everyone else," I said, knowing that I'd had an imaginary conversation with the bird just six weeks before.

When one's parents storm out of the house followed by a psychic who is still holding his missing brother's T-shirt and book, he stands up, looks into his mother's eyes, and wonders where they are headed. He looks over at his best friend, who has tried his best not to cry, and sees that even he seems to be buying into these terrible theatrics. He follows his mother. She turns around, says, "We're going to find your brother," and gets into the backseat of his father's truck. He waves his best friend and Mena Prescott over, lets them get in first, and then squeezes into the crowded backseat while trying to close the door. He gazes out the window as they pass through town. His forehead is smashed flat against the glass.

Book Title #80: *The Looks of Strangers in Stores.*

CHAPTER TWELVE
The Watchers

The librarian told Cabot Searcy that he could find an Ethiopian Orthodox Bible in the section marked Theology, on the seventh floor, and that he was lucky Dr. Sentell had decided to reference the book in one of his divinity courses three semesters before. Cabot smiled at her, nodded his thanks, and waited for the elevator doors to open. Once inside, he reread the small sheet of paper he held in his hand. It read: *The Book of Enoch is found only in the Ethiopian Orthodox Bible. It is a secret writing.*

He had jotted this down after doing an hour's worth of research instead of going to his Human Anatomy lecture that morning. The elevator doors opened. Cabot Searcy was met with silent stares as he walked slowly but confidently to the back corner of the room. He crouched down, scanning row after row of books, his finger gliding lightly over their spines, his eyes bouncing back and forth in his head. When he found what he was looking for, Cabot lugged the thick, heavy book to the nearest table and sat down, looking over his shoulder as if he was doing something secretive or wrong. He opened the book.

The Ethiopian Orthodox Bible is made up of the largest canon of any Bible in print in the modern world. Cabot Searcy, having been raised in a Southern Baptist church in Georgia, had little knowledge of this text before this first encounter. He scanned the table of contents and then opened the book up to I Enoch. This book, referred to more commonly as the Book of Enoch, is split into five major sections, those being the Book of Watchers, the Book of Parables, the Book of the Heavenly Luminaries, the Book of Dream Visions, and the Book of the Epistle of Enoch. Cabot Searcy found himself turning to chapter 10 to read the quote that Benton had left behind. This was in the Book of Watchers, which would serve as the focus of Cabot Searcy's endeavor.

The scripture was highlighted in yellow, causing Cabot to raise one eyebrow as he read word for word the lines that had brought him to the library that morning. And, though highlighted already, the words "angels have corrupted" were also circled in black ink. And farther down the page another line was highlighted and also circled. It read:

And destroy all the spirits of the reprobate and the

children of the Watchers, because they have wronged
mankind.

And even farther down the page another line was marked in
similar ways. It read:

And cleanse thou the earth from all oppression, and
from all unrighteousness, and from all sin, and from
all godlessness: and all the uncleanness that is wrought
upon the earth destroy from off the earth.

And at the bottom of the page there was written something so
small that Cabot Searcy was forced to squint his eyes and bring
his face down as close to the book as possible. He made it out to
read, in cursive and black ink: *The angels taught the humans too*
much. So, what if they hadn't been stopped?

Because Cabot Searcy felt the need to do so, he compared
the words jotted down in the Book of Enoch to the words in
Benton Sage's journal and, to his delight, they seemed to be a
pretty close match. Now Cabot Searcy felt as if he had been
given some sort of posthumous assignment from Benton. Some
righteous mission of discovery. Some quest for the truth behind
existence. Cabot Searcy suddenly found himself consumed by
self-important thoughts as to how he could single-handedly
save mankind.

From reading the Book of Watchers, Cabot began to understand what he believed Benton had written about in his scribbled
note. He read about the fall of the angels, God speaking to Noah,

the Great Flood. He read from his Bible and the Ethiopian one as well. He went back and forth from one to another, Genesis to Enoch. Enoch to Genesis. He read that the angels had taught humans the art of war, had taught them astrology, anatomy. He read that the angels' children became unruly, savage beasts. He began to put the pieces of Benton Sage's puzzle together in his mind. The one thing he'd found in Benton's journal that he'd yet to fit together with the rest of this puzzle was how Benton's vision of God, the angel Gabriel, and some large bird fit into the picture. All he knew was that he had to carry on the work that God had, in the vision, ascribed to Benton. He had to somehow change the world.

"I'll tell you why Noah had to build the ark," Cabot said to his new roommate some time that next semester.

"What?" Chuck Stoppard asked from his bed, where he lay playing a video game.

"The *flood*. I'll tell you why God sent the flood and had Noah build the ark."

"Okay." Chuck Stoppard never looked away from his game.

"It's because we were getting too smart. See, these fallen angels—"

"Fallen angels?" Chuck interrupted.

"That's right. These fallen angels came down, started sleeping with the women here on Earth, and then started teaching us all these things like how to fight and how to understand science and the stars and our bodies, and God looked down and was like, 'Those humans are learning too much from the angels. This has to stop before they get too powerful.' So then he sends Gabriel down to kill the angels, and sooner or later he talks to Noah and sends the flood to kill off all the humans who had gotten too smart."

"Oh," Chuck Stoppard managed.

"Yeah. It's crazy. I know."

"Pretty crazy," Chuck said sarcastically.

"Just think. If Gabriel hadn't stopped them, humans could be so much smarter now. We'd know everything. We'd know how to stop wars, how to cure diseases and all that shit." Cabot flipped through the Bible resting on his chest as he lay in bed.

"Cabot," Chuck Stoppard said from his bed.

"What?"

"I'm an atheist," Chuck said, lying simply to keep from having to hear any more of Cabot Searcy's theories on the potential of humankind.

CHAPTER THIRTEEN
The Simplest Thing in the World

❧ We stood in a field, one where trees had been clear-cut and what remained was nothing more than what looked like some sad, ancient war zone. The grass was mostly dead, the dirt had gone from brown to gray, and the one tree that did still stand was bare and leaning like a creature over a small child's nightmare bed. Vilonia Kline stood before us, her hands outstretched, her eyes closed again, her lips quivering, mumbling something either very important or completely full of shit. Lucas was looking at me the way someone does when a psychic is standing in a field in front of him and talking to the earth. Mena Prescott was now holding my mother's hand, and my father was leaning against the truck, his eyes fixed on the mumbling woman. She walked out about a hundred yards, stopped, and then turned around. Her eyes flew open. Her shoulders jolted back. She put her hands to her sides.

"He is here," she said quietly, but loud enough to be heard, pointing to the ground below her.

"Here"—my mother waved her arms around to encompass the entire field—"or there?" she asked, pointing to the ground beneath Vilonia Kline.

"Here," Vilonia said again, pointing beneath her.

No one, to my surprise, was crying yet. No one was talking, either. Lucas looked over at my father, who looked at me quickly before reaching into the back of his truck and bringing out a shovel. He tossed it onto the ground in front of me. He then brought out another one and propped it against his right shoulder, walking toward the woman. Lucas Cader walked over and grabbed the shovel, looked up at me, and said, "Go sit in the truck." I did, and Mena Prescott went with me. My mother sat on the hood of the truck, watching as they began to dig into the dead earth. Vilonia Kline sat down on the dirt beside them, watching the hole get wider and deeper with each jab and throw.

When one is sitting in the backseat of his father's truck beside his best friend's girlfriend, who has her head resting on his shoulder, and watching as his father and best friend slowly puncture the world to find his little brother, he imagines Vilonia Kline standing up, dusting off her long skirt, and walking down into the hole. He sees her come back out, a dirty, bloodstained T-shirt in her hands. She unwads the shirt, holding it up to her chest the way a mother would hold it up to her child in a clothing store, and it is black, with a big white angel in the center. It is the last shirt that Gabriel Witter was seen wearing. He sees Vilonia Kline gently lay the shirt down on the ground and then walk back down into the hole as they continue to dig around her. She walks back out, now holding a pair of blue jeans, knees stained with grass and dirt, blood caked around the ankles, pockets torn with holes and unraveling. These were the last pants that Gabriel Witter was seen wearing. She sets the jeans gently down under the shirt and begins to walk in a slow circle around the outfit, chanting and holding her hands up in the air. Behind her, from out of the earth, emerges a naked and dirty Gabriel Witter, his hair matted with blood and grime. His skin is clean white in some places but nearly black in others. He turns toward the truck, looks straight at his older brother, and smiles the slightest of smiles.

"I can't believe this!" Vilonia Kline said, frustratingly, to my father as we drove back home.

"What?" my mother asked.

"You didn't dig deep enough. We should go back." Vilonia crossed her arms.

"Ms. Kline, if it's all right with you, could you please not talk for the rest of the ride?" my father said bluntly, dirt smeared across his forehead.

"We must've dug, like, ten feet," Lucas said quietly, sweat still dripping from his nose.

My mother glared at my father the way a wife does, and then

she turned back toward me. She reached one hand back, set it on top of mine, moved it quickly up and down twice, and then turned back around. Mena Prescott was asleep with her head against the window. Lucas Cader was picking dried dirt from the knees of his blue jeans. Vilonia Kline stared out the windshield with her lips tightly shut. She sat between my mother and father like some child on the way to a barbecue. She reminded me of sadness.

Seeing my brother's zombie, or whatever it was, made me think about Russell Quitman and how I probably would never see him again. He was still in Florida, still in a hospital bed, and I was still making out with his ex-girlfriend in the backseat of my mom's car. Ada said to me once, just after we had begun to know each other, that Russell Quitman, though he was a huge asshole, was actually one of the most sensitive people she'd ever known. "He would cry over the strangest things," she said, "like a dead dog on the side of the road or a smell that reminded him of his grandmother."

"Did he cry when you two broke up?" I asked her.

"He wept like a baby."

"Naturally," I joked.

"Wouldn't you?" she said.

"We'll see," I said plainly.

"Ha! What does that mean?"

"We'll just see."

Ada Taylor said that my friendship with Lucas Cader was probably the only thing getting me through all the madness of that summer. Here is more of what I knew about Lucas Cader:

His father was a drunk who used to pay him and his older brother to fight in the front yard. His mother was that sort of woman who rarely speaks and usually says something unintentionally very sad when she does. She let her husband hit her two small children, so I never really took the time to know her. Neither did Lucas. Lucas's father left them in the middle of the night when he was nine years old. Lucas's brother, well on his way to becoming the alcoholic that his father had been, burned to death in a car crash three years after that. Lucas Cader had dated every girl in our grade and most of the ones in our school by the time we were sophomores. He still spent most of his time with me and slept on my floor a good four nights of the week. I loved Lucas Cader, in a very nonsexual way, and this all suited me just fine. And Lucas Cader was as heartbroken over Gabriel as I was, if not more so.

Ada's suggestion, that Lucas was saving me once again, made me wonder what I had ever done for him. I couldn't remember a single time when I helped him out by giving him a ride somewhere or by defending him from some ass-hat punk or by consoling him over the loss of *his* cousin or the disappearance of *his* brother. I couldn't remember Lucas Cader ever needing me for anything save for my unique ability to constantly need rescue from one thing or another.

"Lucas," I said toward the floor from my bed one night.

"Yeah?"

"Why are you my friend?"

"That's a stupid question."

"Why? Because there's no answer?"

"No, because that's like asking why people stretch when they wake up or jump when they're scared," he said sternly.

"Huh?"

"These things just happen, Cullen. You just *are* my friend. That's that. No explanation needed."

"So, you're my friend just because you're my friend?" I laughed.

"That's right. I just am. It's the simplest thing in the world."

Book Title #81: *The Nightmare Bed.*

"Do you remember when Gabriel decided he didn't like toys anymore?" Mom said to me one morning in that I'm-talking-about-the-past-and-being-eerily-nostalgic sort of way.

"Yeah."

"We bagged up all those action figures. There must have been, I don't know, a hundred of those things," she said.

"At least," I added.

"I think we sold about twenty of 'em in a bag for fifty cents at that garage sale. And he didn't cry a wink. He was ready, I guess."

"Ready for what?" I asked.

"Ready to be grown," she answered.

"I guess so."

"You never played with toys much when you were young. You were always out in the yard making up these strange scenarios and fightin' imaginary pirates and monsters. It was the cutest thing."

"Yeah?" I asked.

"Like watching someone with multiple personalities," she said, laughing.

"Thanks, Mom."

Before Lucas Cader moved to Lily and became my friend, I spent most of my time either with my brother or completely alone. Gabriel, though, didn't really like going outside or swimming or anything like that. He liked to stay in, read books, watch TV, and pretend that he was grown up. I never wanted to feel grown up, to be like an adult. I wanted to scream until it hurt my throat and made me talk funny for the rest of the day, and I wanted to run through my neighbor's sprinklers and track mud into the house and shake my wet hair like a dog would in the middle of the living room. In church, I used to try and get my brother to play tic-tac-toe on the bulletin, but he always refused, shushing me and pointing to the preacher. My brother once told me that God was like the best musician in the world, because he put together all the sounds of nature and gave people like Jimi Hendrix his fingers and John Lennon his brain.

"And he's the best writer, too," Gabriel said to me.

"Why's that?" I asked.

"Because he gives every good writer something to struggle with and try to work out by writing it down. That's genius."

My brother stood at about five-eleven and had brown, shaggy hair. He never used a comb, but always just dried his hair furiously with a towel until it seemed to all fall down in the right places. He usually wore some band T-shirt or a shirt that he'd found at a thrift store or something. I never remember seeing him in any pants other than his faded blue jeans or his brown Dickies, which I think were meant to be work pants. He did not skateboard and he never once even tried to play the guitar. His eyes were about like mine, blue not like the sky but like plastic Easter eggs. He had dimples, too, just like mine, and if it hadn't been for his somewhat thicker eyebrows and smaller nose, we would have been able to pass for twins. Because I was just about one inch shorter than him and my uncle Joseph had died, Gabriel was the tallest member of my entire family.

Since he had been gone, I had taken to wearing my brother's T-shirts almost every day. I'm not sure exactly what compelled me to do so, but then again, I'm not sure exactly what ever compelled me to do or say any of the things I did and said back then. Because my brother didn't have any friends except for Libby Truett, I decided to visit her one afternoon seven weeks after he'd been missing. The last time I'd seen her was a couple of weeks earlier, when she was sitting in front of me in church and, turning around slowly, had asked me how I was doing. During the preacher's sermon, she drew a picture of an aardvark and passed it back to me.

Knock-knock.

The door opened and Libby stood before me, her hair pulled back in a ponytail and her green eyes fixed on my face. She looked surprised, but not in that I-can't-believe-you-are-at-my-house sort of way. It was more like *Oh, Cullen, please don't tell me bad news.*

"Cullen!" she said enthusiastically.

"Libby, how are you, my darling?" I said, because I always called Libby Truett my darling.

"I'm fine," she said, laughing. "Come in, please."

She stepped aside, holding the door open for me, and followed me into the living room, where I took a seat on the pale green sofa. She sat across from me in a recliner that seemed unable to stop rocking back and forth after she'd sat down. It squeaked, too, and as we stared at each other and waited for the other to speak, it was beginning to annoy me.

"Are you still working at the store?" she asked me.

"Oh yeah. I'm sure I'll be there for the next forty years or so," I joked.

"Been thinking about college much? I heard Lucas was goin' to U of A, you goin' with him?"

"I'm not sure yet. Maybe. Maybe not. I can't seem to ever think about it too long without getting a headache," I answered.

"Yeah. It's a big decision, I guess."

"Yeah. And we know I'm not good at those."

I wasn't sure when exactly to bring up my brother to Libby, who I assumed was thinking the same thing. We talked for a while longer about whether or not I was going to study writing or just be like everyone else who wanted to be a writer and become a teacher instead. I told her that I didn't have the patience to be a teacher, and she began to talk about how she had briefly considered going to nursing school but couldn't bear to be around blood. It was the mention of blood that, sadly, brought us to talking about Gabriel.

"Can you try not to cry?" I asked Libby as nicely as I could manage.

"I can try," she answered, nearly laughing.

"Okay. Thanks."

"You're not going to either, are you?" Libby asked me.

"I rarely do."

"So, what did you want to talk to me about?"

"Was my brother happy?" I asked her bluntly.

"What do you mean?"

"Was he happy?" I said again.

"He seemed it."

"He seemed it to me, too, but was he *really* happy?"

"I think he was as happy as a fifteen-year-old in Lily can be. I think he wasn't unhappy, just content, ya know?" Libby said, picking at her fingernails.

"Are you happy?" I asked her.

"I was." Her face turned pale. Her eyes lost life. Her tone changed to that of a girl trying not to start crying.

It was at that point that I had to, contrary to my normal behavior, hug my brother's best friend. What you need to know about me is that I don't like to hug people with whom I'm not romantically involved. I also don't really like to shake people's hands, sit close enough to touch someone else, or feel other people's breath on my skin. If you're the type of person who likes to do any of those things, then I won't pretend to understand you. Libby was tougher than I had imagined she'd be, never once breaking down or even shedding the first tear. She hugged me tightly, her face pressed firmly against my neck, and sat there still and quiet until I finally patted her twice on the back the way a boy does when he is ready to stop hugging.

When one is driving home from Libby Truett's house and

there is nothing worth listening to on the radio, he imagines his little brother sitting on the floor of Libby's room and trying to convince her to kiss him. He sees Gabriel lean in and, gently resting his hand on Libby's knee, close his eyes and wait for her to meet his lips. He imagines Gabriel flushed with embarrassment when nothing happens, standing up and then sitting as far away as possible and trying not to look up at her. He sees Libby walk across the room, wrap her arms around Gabriel's neck, and squeeze him tightly. He hears her say she loves him. He hears Gabriel say it back. His brother, he thinks, was in love with everyone he knew.

My mother does this thing when she is cutting someone's hair where she sticks half her tongue out of her mouth, the tip of which is folded back behind her lips like she is biting down on her tongue and forcing the leftovers out. Had Gabriel been sitting beside me on that afternoon in the salon as I witnessed her doing this, he would have quickly said, "Mom, tongue," and she would have, with a slightly embarrassed look on her face, coiled her tongue back into her mouth and continued spraying Mrs. Elmore's hair.

Similarly, when my dad focuses on something, he bites his lower lip and squints his eyes, as if to suggest that whatever he's doing is extremely complex. He does this while making pancakes, changing the oil in my mom's car, or reading the morning paper. He was also doing this on the day that Agent Perry sat across from us on the couch to talk about the investigation.

"We are following up on a few leads, but to tell the truth, we're pretty sure they're dead ends."

"Dead ends," my dad repeated back, also something he did when focusing.

"Yeah. We've exhausted our resources, Sam. We've followed every lead, every phone call, every letter. This is just a tough one." Agent Perry's face was filled with sincere disappointment.

"Y'all have done a great job, Mr. Perry. We're just trying to stay hopeful, ya know? We're still positive about this," my dad said.

"Sam," my mom said, looking at my dad as if he'd slapped her, "they haven't done a damn thing."

"Sarah, please. They've done what they can do. We thank them for their efforts," he said, nodding toward Agent Perry and wrapping an arm around Mom.

"Well, ma'am, this case is not closed by any means. We've got several of our best agents assigned to it and we, too, believe it or not, are very hopeful. But I've done all I can do here."

"We know, we know," my dad said as my mother's eyes welled with tears and I stood quietly at her side.

"You've all been so kind to our crew. We appreciate it. Under other circumstances, I would have very much enjoyed my stay here in Lily," Agent Perry said, standing up to shake my dad's hand.

We walked, my parents and I, with Agent Perry out to his car, and as he backed out of the driveway, we all seemed to have the same sort of look about us: one of disillusionment and lightness. It was that sort of feeling in your head when you think about how the air feels on your skin and how the sidewalk sounds under your feet. It was the kind of feeling that makes you jump at the touch of your mother's hand on the back of your neck as you step onto the porch. Less a state of mind and more a physical reaction to something. This was our physical reaction to my brother's case seeming completely unsolvable.

Lucas Cader's first response when I told him about Agent Perry's visit was to walk over to the store's freezer, open it up, and stick his head inside. After a few seconds, Lucas walked back over to the counter where I stood, and said that this meant nothing. We didn't hug or say anything else that you would expect to hear in this strange sort of daytime soap opera moment, but instead we began to laugh and continued on with a detailed discussion of Ada Taylor's intentions with me that we'd begun that morning at breakfast.

"So, do you think she really likes you, or is it all just for sympathy?" Lucas asked.

"I think she really likes me. But that's what I really want, so I dunno."

"I think it's real. She doesn't seem the type to play games."

"Yeah. She's pretty straightforward," I agreed.

"Cullen, I'm just glad you're not dead yet," he said, laughing.

"Well, I have been avoiding cars and the river, just in case," I joked back.

"So, does she ever mention those guys? All of that mess. The rumors?" he asked.

"Just once. One day at the park, we were on the swing set, and she asked me if I was scared of her."

"What'd you say?" Lucas asked.

"I said, 'Why would I be?'"

"And?"

"And she said, 'Because I'm cursed.'"

"Cursed," Lucas whispered, as if he'd had a revelation of some kind.

"Yeah, and I couldn't tell whether she was being serious or joking, because her next move was to lean over and kiss me on the cheek. I dunno. She's hard to read."

It was then that Lucas Cader suggested we all go out that Friday night, him and Mena, me and Ada. It would be "awesome," as he put it. Lucas uses the word "awesome" when he's trying to convince me to do something he knows I don't want to do. Cleaning his room and working on his transmission are also "awesome." And so we planned it, and I was all ready to go that evening when the phone rang and my mom tossed it toward me in the kitchen.

"Cullen?" Ada said from the other end.

"Yeah?"

"Did you sleep with Alma Ember?" she asked plainly.

"What?" I said, stunned.

"Did you, Cullen? Just tell me. It's not a big deal, I just need to know."

"Yes," I said, feeling as if I had little to lose.

"Okay. Umm, are you almost ready?"

"Yeah, Lucas is just pulling up, we'll be there in five."

"Okay. Bye."

"Bye."

Click.

At the drive-in, which is where the sober teenagers in Lily went on Friday nights, we all waited in line for popcorn and swatted away mosquitoes. I was trying my best to watch the previews while Ada kept asking me questions about Alma Ember. Lucas looked at me from the corner of his eye; he was amused. So was Mena, who kept trying to use her unique ability to never shut up to egg Ada on with her questioning.

"Were you two in love?" Ada whispered in my ear.

"No, Ada," I said back.

"Did she love you?"

"Ada, I don't know. Leave it alone." I was getting angry.

"I'm sorry," she said.

"No. It's fine. Just, can we talk later?" I asked, turning to face her.

"Yeah."

The movie was just interesting enough to stay focused on until Ada took it upon herself to start making out with me. This was the other thing teenagers in Lily did on Friday nights—Lucas and Mena were engaged in the same sort of behavior in the front seat. It was when she tried to take my shirt off that I asked Ada to take a walk with me. Once we'd reached the top of a nearby hill, I sat down on the dirt. She sat down beside me.

"Ada," I said.

"Yeah?"

"I need to know what this is."

"What what is?"

"This. Us," I said.

"Isn't it better not knowing? Like, just liking each other and seeing each other all the time without any definition to it?"

"No?" I said dumbly.

"Cullen, are you in love with me?" she blurted out.

"Umm." I struggled to come up with something to say that wasn't a lie.

"Are you?" she asked again.

"Yes?" I said, as if asking her permission.

"You're not," she said, beginning to laugh.

"Huh?"

"You just lied to me," she said, standing up in front of me.

"Ada, what's it matter? We've just been going out for a couple of weeks. Quit being so serious," I joked, in an attempt to distract from my own melodramatic ways.

"You're the serious one. You're the one with lies and secret hookups all over town. What happened to innocent Cullen Witter?"

"Who?" I joked.

"The gas station boy who stared at me through the window?"

"Oh. I guess he died."

"That's not funny," she said, sitting back down.

"I thought it was," I said, leaning my head down on her shoulder.

"You're a jerk," she said.

"I'm the nicest guy you've ever met, and you know it."

"Even so," she said, "you're still a jerk."

Waking up in Ada Taylor's house was nothing like doing the same thing in Alma Ember's. Ada whispered, "Get up, get up," into my ear as I stretched my arms and legs and let out a groan. I sat up, my contacts glued to my eyes, the air conditioner blowing uncomfortably onto my face.

"You have to leave now," Ada whispered.

"How?" I whispered back. "I don't have a car."

"You'll walk. I don't know."

"Walk? It's, like, four miles," I said, breaking my whisper.

"Shhh. You'll wake my mom up."

"What time is it?" I asked, returning to my whisper.

"It's five thirty."

"A.M.?"

"Yes. Now get up!"

"Okay, okay."

When one is sneaking out the window of the girl he just slept with, he immediately remembers all the movies in which he'd seen this very thing happen and thought about how these things never happen in real life. He begins to laugh until he realizes that there is no way on Earth he can walk the four miles home. He thinks momentarily about calling his father, who would be the only person in town awake at that hour, but dismisses the idea after trying to come up with an explanation to give him. "Umm, Dad, I just had to sneak out of a girl's house," he says to himself as he walks down the sidewalk and past a house with plastic lawn ornaments of geese and deer. Then, no surprise, he decides to call Lucas Cader to save him one more time. This seems the easiest solution until, stopped in his tracks, he remembers that he has no phone and that turning around and crawling back through Ada Taylor's window is out of the question. He thinks of knocking on someone's front door and making up some sob story about being stranded but knows that he would never go through with it. And so, with a better attitude than most about something he really can't change, Cullen Witter walks down the street and is home an hour and fifteen minutes later.

The thing that bothered me most about my little brother was the way he constantly corrected everyone's grammar. If you used a word even barely wrong he would be there to catch it, correct you, and then explain to you why you had made the mistake, even though you probably weren't listening. But oddly enough, I found myself missing these corrections that summer. I would be sitting in my room and, out loud, say to no one things like, "Neither of us are going" and "I laid down for a nap this afternoon." And then I would listen to the silence that was not my brother fixing my mistakes and I would pretend, just for a moment, to be him. "Neither of us *is* going," I would say smugly. "I *lay* down for a nap this afternoon."

I did not talk to Ada Taylor for three days after being practically thrown out of her house. I didn't call her, she didn't call me. It was as if we'd at some point planned to not call each other for that set period of time, because when I finally decided to drive over to her house, I nearly backed into her pulling up into our driveway. We leaned against her car, her talking, me listening. She said things like, "Sorry, but Mom is really strict, and she'd kill me if she knew I had a boy stay over," and "I think my dad might have heard us whispering, but I don't think he'll say anything."

"Next time," she said, "we'll just have to find a better place."

"Right," I said, unable to restrain my smile.

"You perv," she joked, punching me in the arm.

"Your mom's a perv."

"That's mature."

"Your mom's mature." I laughed.

"Cullen."

"Sorry."

Book Title #82: *Five A.M. Is for Lovers and Lawn Ornaments.*

CHAPTER FOURTEEN
Alma Ember and Her Small-Town Ways

❦   When she decided to move in with her grandmother in Savannah, Alma Ember had to make only one phone call before she was sent a one-way plane ticket and cab fare in a brown manila envelope. Upon her arrival, she was greeted at the door by Beverly Ember, who looked nowhere near her age, which was supposedly seventy-six. Her grandmother hugged her neck, her strong perfume nearly choking Alma, and swayed back and forth until finally letting go, leaning back to look at Alma's face, and then going in for another hug.

"You look so beautiful," she said to her only granddaughter.

"I get it from you," Alma said back, smiling.

It took little time for Alma to settle in, and she eventually got used to her grandmother's constant questions and suggestions about what they should do or where they should go. Alma had decided, at the last minute, not to accept the fully paid scholarship offered to her by the University of Arkansas, and opted instead to attend the Savannah College of Art and Design, where she would finally stop talking about being a photographer and become one. All of this, of course, was afforded to her by Beverly Ember, who had, upon the death of her third husband, reached a financial status she'd never before thought possible. And so Alma Ember began her studies and lived with her grandmother in the mostly peaceful Georgia town, allowing herself to be troubled only by portfolio deadlines and country-club luncheons.

Her freshman year proved more challenging than she'd hoped, but Alma walked out on the last day of the semester with an A average and a long, steady stride, her hair in a swinging ponytail, her green and white skirt bouncing at her every step. When she got home, she kissed her grandmother's cheek, walked up the stairs to her room, and tossed her book bag into the bottom of her closet. She threw herself back onto her bed and, still bouncing slightly, let her limbs fall lifeless to her sides. She closed her eyes. She took a deep breath. She fell asleep.

Upon graduating with his degree in philosophy, Cabot Searcy was told by his father that he couldn't have wasted more money or time if he'd tried. Cabot grinned at this, leaned close to his father's right ear, and told him to wait and see. Over the three years since Benton Sage had died, Cabot had continued his study of the Book of Enoch, and had even written four research papers on the topic. Cabot Searcy would not give up his "quest," as he called it, for the truth behind modern human existence. He had debated exhaustingly with theology majors, had butted heads with two or three local pastors, and had once been involved in a fist fight after calling the president of the Catholic Students Foundation an ignorant pedophile. There were many people very glad to see Cabot Searcy—who had begun his college years as a charming, friendly, and polite young man—leaving for good.

"Well, what now?" Cabot's uncle Jeff asked him after the graduation ceremony, as the family gathered in a restaurant near downtown Atlanta.

"Well, I was thinking about graduate school, but I'm not sure which one," Cabot answered.

"What area of study are you considering this time?" his aunt Corinne asked.

"I was thinking about finding a place to study ancient theology."

"Are you going to be a minister?" one of his sisters asked.

"No," he answered.

"How is it," his father began, "that you plan on ever making any money, Cabot?"

"I'll get by," he said plainly.

"Not on my dollar, you won't," his father said quietly.

"Richard," Cabot's mom whispered, glaring at her husband from across the table.

"Well," Uncle Jeff said, raising his glass, "how about a toast?"

"To what?" his wife asked.

"To Cabot finding his way."

Clink.

Alma Ember didn't like going out on dates. In fact, she hated the very thought of sitting awkwardly across from some guy she'd just met and pretending to be interested in what he said or racking her brain to say things to make herself seem interesting to him. And so she just avoided the whole thing altogether. She declined offers to go get coffee; she froze up at the first inclination of flirtation. She sat away from any guy who showed her too much attention in class. Living with a seventy-six-year-old was beginning to take its toll on Alma, however, as the summer moved slowly along and she grew tired of sitting poolside alone at the country club and watching senior citizens drink martinis.

The first date that Alma agreed to go on since arriving in Savannah one year earlier was with a twenty-two-year-old graphic design major named Nico. Nico, whom she'd met in her design class, was from Aspen, Colorado. He had looked her number up and had given her a call sometime that June. She briefly considered letting him down, but took a deep breath, shook her head, and told him she was free for Friday night.

They ate on the balcony of a nice restaurant. Alma only felt uncomfortable one time, and only because the waiter kept flirting with her. Nico looked better than he had in class, mostly because he was wearing a nice button-down instead of some wrinkly T-shirt. He did the things that girls like to have done for them on first dates. Opened doors. Pulled back chairs. Gave random compliments. Laughed at her jokes. Didn't laugh at his own. He never broke eye contact with her. He was confident, but not cocky. Suave, but eccentrically charming. He spoke without flaw about things like art and music, and always asked her opinions and listened to her answers. He nodded his head. He took small sips of his water. He stood up when she left to go to the restroom.

In the mirror, Alma Ember practiced her smile. She said something like, "Of course I'll marry you," while batting her eyelids. She began to make herself laugh. She washed her hands, reapplied her lipstick, and walked toward the table. After they both sat back down, Nico asked her a question.

"Why do you want to be a photographer?"

"That's hard. I'm not sure. It just seems right," she answered.

"Right. It seems like what you were made for, you mean?" he asked.

"It's like every time I see something beautiful, I wish I had it on film. And this is my way of making sure that every thing like that is captured somehow," she said, lighting up at her own surprising response.

"Awesome," he said, taking another sip of water.

"And you?" she asked.

"Me what?" he said, smiling.

"Why do you want to be a graphic designer?"

"The money," he answered plainly.

"What?" She laughed.

"Oh, and it's fun, too." He laughed with her.

In the three weeks that followed, Alma Ember stayed over at Nico's apartment every night but two, causing her grandmother to suspect that she was being corrupted and leading to a brief argument about proper ladylike behavior.

"Ladies don't stay over at men's homes," Beverly said.

"There's nothing wrong with it, Grandmother," she said back.

"It just doesn't look good to me."

"You don't trust me?" Alma asked, her eyes big and watery.

"Of course I do, honey. I just worry, you know that."

"I know. I'll try and do better," Alma said, biting lettuce off her fork.

One week later, Alma asked her grandmother if Nico could move into the guest bedroom for a few weeks until he found a new apartment. His roommate had left him with rent that he couldn't afford. Beverly sighed deeply, looked up at Alma, and nodded yes. One month later, Nico sat on the couch in the living room as Beverly poured herself an iced tea in the kitchen and Alma whispered to her mother on the phone in her bedroom.

"Mom, I'm getting married next month."

Cabot Searcy's uncle Jeff had hired him to run errands for his real estate development company that summer, and Cabot, although he found the job to be boring and tedious, enjoyed being able to live in his uncle's large house and spend his free time reading and writing. What he also liked about Savannah was the quietness of the place, the lack of traffic, the sweet tea, and the way his aunt's friends talked and laughed when they gathered in the parlor to play Uno. After about a month of this, Cabot had a conversation with his father on the telephone.

"You can't just live off your uncle for the rest of your life, Cabot," his father said.

"I know that, Dad. I've been looking for jobs and stuff," he replied.

"Where? What jobs have you looked for?"

"Umm, well, I looked at the want ads and didn't see anything," Cabot said.

"You've got to start taking things seriously. This is ridiculous." His father was beginning to raise his voice.

"Dad, give me some time. I'll figure it out. I know you're frustrated and so am I, but it'll just take time."

Cabot's cousin, Josh, who was still in high school, walked into his bedroom one afternoon and sat down on the bed. He picked at the bedspread before looking over at Cabot, who sat at the desk in the corner, and began to speak.

"Can you do me a favor?" he asked.

"What is it?" Cabot replied.

"Do you think you could take me to the movies tonight?" Josh asked hesitantly.

"Sure. No problem. I got nothing else to do."

"Thanks," Josh said, springing up, smiling, and walking out of the room.

In the movie theater, Cabot and Josh sat in the back row, popcorn in one hand and a six-dollar drink in the other. They each put their feet up on the empty seat in front of them and leaned back, waiting for the lights to dim and the movie to start.

"So, is this supposed to be funny?" Cabot asked Josh.

"I think some of it is. It's like part funny and part sad," Josh answered.

"I've never heard of it before now," Cabot said.

"I hear it's great."

The lights dimmed in the movie theater as Alma and Nico situated themselves in their seats near the front row. They had walked in just in time—not too late to miss the beginning of the movie, but just late enough to miss the opportunity for decent seats. Nico seemed unaffected by this. Alma was angered, whispering into his ear, "I'm gonna need a chiropractor after this." Nico chuckled as the previews began to light up the screen, and Alma continued to gripe about the seats, spilling half her popcorn in the process and then quietly closing her eyes for a few seconds to calm down.

Thirty-seven minutes into the movie was all it took Alma Ember to realize that she was not yet ready to force herself to enjoy some indie snore-fest just because it was the only thing Nico liked to watch. She whispered into his ear that she needed to use the restroom and scooted her way out of the row of seats. Once back in the lobby, she sat down on a bench and picked tiny bits of popcorn off her shirt. She took out her phone and tried to call the first friend she could think of to make fun of the terrible movie. She got no answer. As she attempted to call a second friend to kill more time, someone sat down beside her, muttering something under his breath.

"What?" she said, looking up at the young man, his hair disheveled and in his eyes, his skin tan and his expression bored.

"I can't sit through any more of that shit," he said, laughing.

"You too?" she asked.

"It's like watching a car wreck or something," he joked.

"More like getting a root canal," she joked back.

"I'm Cabot," he said.

"Alma," she said, grasping and shaking his outstretched hand.

"I have an aunt named Alma," he said.

"I know a town named Cabot," she said back.

"Is that right?" he asked.

"Little place in Arkansas."

"That's where you're from?" he said excitedly.

"Yeah, a little town called Lily."

"I knew you sounded southern, but not quite from Georgia."

"Good ears," she said.

"Thanks."

It took two days to move all of Nico's things out of Beverly's house, even with a couple of his friends helping him. He stood mostly in the corner of the room, still shocked and confused by Alma's quick decision to break off their engagement and ask him to leave. Alma had planned to be out of the house and instead was with Cabot Searcy, playing golf and talking about her aspirations to become a wildlife photographer. Cabot shared with her his philosophies about life and even a little bit of his theory concerning the potential of humankind. She marveled at his speech, completely enamored by the things he said and did. He wasn't trying to act perfect, something Nico did regularly. He had little shame over mooching off his uncle and even less about his useless college degree. He seemed carefree to Alma, and that was what she desired to be. To Cabot, Alma Ember seemed just innocent enough to be loved but adventurous enough not to bore the hell out of everyone.

"Is it positive?" Cabot asked her through the bathroom door one and a half months later.

"Can you wait just one minute and I'll show you?" Alma shouted back.

After a few minutes she opened the door, and as Cabot stood up to face her, she began to cry. Her head fell flat against his chest and he wrapped his arms around her. They stayed like this for a while. Cabot could see the white stick sitting on the edge of the counter, a bold blue check in its center. He could not help but smile as Alma cried.

"We'll get married," he said to her hours later as they lay in bed.

"We can't just get married, just like that," she said back.

"And why not?" he asked.

"We've only been dating for a little over a month. What will people think?"

"Well, Alma, what will they think when you're walking around with a baby in your stomach? That it's the second coming?" He laughed.

"Not funny," she said, trying not to grin.

"Tomorrow we'll go get the license. It's the right thing to do," he said, kissing her cheek.

"Tomorrow then," she agreed.

CHAPTER FIFTEEN
Aunt Julia and the Love Parade

❧   My mother was born ten min-
utes before my aunt Julia, who seemed to have become some
sort of a recluse that summer, rarely leaving her house and,
according to my mom, "stinking to high heaven." Before, when
Oslo wasn't dead and Gabriel wasn't probably dead, Aunt Julia
would drop in for uninvited chats in the kitchen with Mom
while my dad's eyes rolled and my brother and I tried to stay
hidden in our rooms. Before, she would have brought over
homemade cookies and a cold chicken casserole for my dad,
along with explicit instructions on how to properly heat it up.
She would have talked and talked and talked, mostly about
people we didn't know or didn't like, and would, upon asking

you a question, quickly interrupt you and continue on with her own thoughts. One such visit, when I was around fifteen, resulted in a conversation that went something like this:

"Cullen," my mom said to me as Aunt Julia backed out of the driveway.

"What?"

"Did you see what just happened here?" she asked.

"No."

"You see, my dear. Your mother is very astute. I have finally learned how to shut that woman up," she said, pointing to Aunt Julia's car as it bounced down the road.

"How?" I asked.

"Well, it's not so hard. It's all about timing, really."

"What is it, Mom?"

"All you have to do is wait for a sudden pause, which you know will be hard to find when Aunt Julia is on a roll, and then you just open your mouth and don't stop, no matter what."

"What do you say, though?" I asked.

"Anything. But try to make it something that doesn't involve your aunt at all. Like you could talk about school or a TV show you just watched. Just as long as you talk for a few minutes without letting her have any time to say anything back."

"Then what happens?"

"Well, then your aunt Julia suddenly snaps up and remembers somewhere she has to be or someone she has promised to visit. It's rude, you're probably thinking, but it's the only way."

Now, with Oslo gone, my mother had taken to visiting her sister on a daily basis, usually right after she left the salon, and would most often take Julia a sandwich or burger from some-where, knowing she probably hadn't eaten that day. It was one Saturday, a day that I had surprisingly not been put on the schedule to work at the store, that my mother called home and I answered.

"Hello."

"Cullen?"

"Hey, Mom."

"Can you do me a favor?" she asked in that way that implied that saying no would cause someone to die.

"I guess. I mean, I don't have to go anywhere, do I?"

"I just need you to go by Burke's or somewhere like that and pick up a cheeseburger and some fries and take it over to your aunt's house. Can you do that for me?"

"You can't do it on your way home?" I asked.

"I'm swamped down here. I know she's probably waiting for some food. Please just go."

"Fine."

"Good. Love ya."

"You too."

Click.

I could not convince Lucas, who had a strange fear of my aunt, to go with me to her house, and because I had my own odd fear of waking people up, I dared not mess with my dad, who had fallen asleep on the couch watching *Wheel of Fortune*, which he was no good at anyway. So I very carefully picked up his keys from the coffee table and tiptoed through the living room and out the door. I hated driving my dad's too-wide truck, which made one feel as if he were driving in both lanes at once. I pulled through Burke's, got Aunt Julia a Number Three with fries, and headed toward her house.

Aunt Julia was wearing a silk nightgown, and I followed her into the dining room while wondering if that same nightgown had belonged to my dead grandmother. Aunt Julia sat down at her table, and I sat down beside her and watched as she devoured the cheeseburger like a lion eating a zebra. I stared at her wood-paneled walls, her light pink curtains, her statue of a golden owl in the corner. I rocked lightly from left to right in the chair and pretended that the fake bird chirping her clock made when it struck six hadn't scared me.

"You want some fries?" she asked with a mouth full of food.

"No thanks. I ate earlier."

"I just don't think I can eat all these."

"Well, you don't have to. Just throw them away," I said.

"No, that's silly. Here, have some." She pushed the fries over to me.

"No, I'm good. Not hungry."

"Eat a damn fry, Cullen!" she yelled. I picked up a fry and tossed it into my mouth.

Aunt Julia watched me intently as I continued to eat. I said nothing, because that's what I do when someone yells at me, and I wondered whether she was going to do it again. I just kept picking up one fry after another and tossing them into my mouth, chewing slowly but not too slowly and staring down at the shiny wooden tabletop. Then I felt her hand rest heavily on top of mine, and when I looked up I saw that she was smiling.

I smiled back. Aunt Julia got up and walked through the living room and into her bedroom. I waited there for about ten minutes, and right as I was about to walk out the door, Aunt Julia walked back into the room.

"Cullen, ya know, it just isn't right that we should all be left here to rot like this."

"What?" I asked.

"Us. Me, you, your mom, your dad. Here we are, all of us good enough people. All of us living our lives, not hurtin' a soul. And here we are left behind in this godforsaken place called Earth to do what?" She paused and stared at me.

"Is that rhetorical or do you want me to answer?" I asked.

"To sit here and rot like we're some sorta animals. They all expect us to pretend that it's okay and that it's gonna be all right. Well, it's not. Nothin's all right anymore. I hate this house. I hate this town. I hate the damn mailman who keeps peeking through my front window!" She stretched her neck toward the porch.

"Aunt Julia, please," I said calmly.

"Please what?"

"Please just sit down for a minute," I said to her, walking over and putting an arm around her shoulder.

"I can do that myself, Cullen. I'm not old, I'm pissed off."

"I know. I know."

We sat across from each other, she in a recliner and me on the couch, which I'm pretty sure she'd slept on for weeks. Aunt Julia had gotten dressed; had put on a nice outfit, a lacy blouse and skirt; and had attempted to put on makeup, though it was obvious she'd done this quickly; her attempt at making me a more comfortable guest. I sat up in my seat, resting my elbows on my knees. I looked at my aunt and remembered that she used to be pretty.

"Why don't you just come stay with us for a while?" I said to her.

"Because y'all got enough to deal with."

"It wouldn't be a problem," I said.

"It would for me, okay?" she said back.

"Well, you've been through a lot, and it just makes sense for you not to be out here all alone, that's all."

"Cullen, no matter what y'all do, I'll always be all alone. A dead husband, a dead son. Then there's me. Ole Julia"—she began to get louder—"the queen of Sherwood Drive!"

"Are you on medication?" I asked bluntly, that being the first time I had ever had the nerve.

"Honey, I got more chemicals in me than a bottle of dishwashing liquid." She laughed, and loudly, I might add.

"Gabriel used to say that you were the best cook in the world, did you know that?" I said.

"Did he?" She looked at the floor.

"Yeah. We used to fight over your cookies. And Dad would always come in and say, 'Now, now, the only way to settle this is for me to eat the last one,' and then he'd snatch it before we could stop him." I laughed.

"Is that right?" she asked.

"That's right. Have you been cooking much lately?" I asked, knowing the answer.

"Cullen, does it look like I've been doing anything lately?"

"Not really."

"Then why ask?"

"Well, why not get back in the kitchen, then?" I said with fake enthusiasm.

"I forgot how to do it all. It's been so long. I think what I need is to get ready for bed, and maybe you could just get that light right there"—she pointed to the kitchen switch—"on your way out."

"You'll call if you need anything?" I asked.

"I'll call, baby."

I had never before felt compelled to turn around and hug my aunt, but something made me do it, the same thing that makes people hold doors open for old ladies at the grocery store or stop and let people cross the road; things that felt regular and impersonal to those doing them, but meant the world to those on the receiving end. I wrapped my arms around her and held her to my chest. It was very quiet in the room, I remember because I could hear Aunt Julia's breathing. As I walked out the door, she stood watching me from the living room, her arms limp at her sides, her shoulders slumped over, her face only half alive.

Book Title #83: *The Mailman Always Peeps Twice.*

Lucas Cader walked into my bedroom and sat down beside me on the floor the afternoon after my aunt Julia forced me to eat french fries. He had a grin on his face, but not the same kind of grin that he would have had before Gabriel left. This was sort of a forced elation, which we all seemed to be getting pretty good at.

"What is it?" I asked finally.

"I have big news from town."

"What is it?"

"They got a picture of the bird this morning."

"No way," I said, almost actually interested.

"Yeah. John Barling, that son of a bitch, went out before the ass crack of dawn and swears up and down that he has a photo of a real live, living, breathing Lazarus woodpecker."

"Well, I'll be damned, Lucas. Stop the presses, the world's gonna be all right after all!" I said comically, standing up and slapping my knee.

"What I heard is that they're going to unveil it at the festival next weekend," Lucas said, standing up as well.

"Festival?"

"Oh, don't tell me you haven't heard about Lily's own Woodpecker Festival!" Lucas shouted, slapping me on the back.

"You've got to be—"

"Nope. I'm dead serious. It's in the paper, Cullen. Do you ever leave this room?"

"Not anymore."

"You working today?"

"I quit."

"You did what?" Lucas sat down on my bed.

"I called Ted this morning and I told him I wanted to quit."

"Was he mad?" Lucas asked.

"No. He was all 'I understand, son. You've been through a lot lately,' and shit like that."

"And your mom? Your dad?" Lucas asked.

"They're too preoccupied to notice. Let's keep it that way, okay?"

"Fine, but why'd you quit?" he kept on.

"Because every person who walks into the store isn't my brother, and I can't keep looking up every time that door goes *ding* and being disappointed."

"Oh. Okay. Well, what now?"

"What now? Well, I'm gonna sit in this room until someone better-looking than you comes to pick me up, and then hopefully she's gonna remind me of why I have hands and a mouth," I said, half-seriously.

"You mean Ada, right?"

"Right."

"She's at Russell's," Lucas said, his expression nervous.

"The Quit Man's?"

"Thought you were gonna stop calling him that," Lucas stated plainly.

Every morning I would hear from my bedroom window the sound of John Barling slamming the Dumases' front door, letting the screen door shut (*tap tap tap*), and, a few seconds later, cranking up his monstrosity of a truck and backing out the gravel drive. Fulton Dumas informed me one awkward day in the yard that John Barling had been sleeping in the guest room for some two and a half weeks. He also said that Barling stayed up all hours of the night, usually in the kitchen, flipping through books, listening to audio recordings of birdcalls, and speaking his notes into a handheld tape recorder. Fulton Dumas said that if John Barling didn't find that bird soon and leave, he would personally slit his throat as he slept.

"Why wait?" I asked him, laughing.

"My mom used to think he was brilliant," he answered. "I think she wants him to find the bird even though she hates his guts now."

"Is he brilliant, you think?" I asked.

"He's maybe the dumbest person I've ever met."

Dr. Webb says that people like John Barling will always be looking for something, whether it's a two-foot-tall woodpecker or the meaning of life; they are simply born and stay incomplete. And when I thought about it enough, I decided that maybe everyone I knew was looking for something in different ways. Lucas Cader looked for his lost brother in everyone he met, but in Gabriel and me in particular. Aunt Julia would, from then on, look for Oslo in the people she met. And likewise, I assumed that my mom and dad would always look for Gabriel, both literally and figuratively speaking. And as for myself, well, I was still trying to find out who I was back then. Trying to figure out why I said and did the things I said and did. Trying to understand why I cried ten minutes after Lucas told me Ada was at Russell's but never shed a tear when my cousin dropped dead. Wondering why I had written nearly ninety titles, but not one single book. Questioning why I couldn't do a damn thing to bring my brother back, no matter how often I sat and tried to think of ways to do so.

When one is sitting on the floor of his bedroom and waiting

for a girl to show up who might not show up at all, he begins to remember the last time he sat in church with his little brother. He remembers that after Reverend Wells's sermon, the congregation began a discussion on the remaining funds needed to complete various and largely unnecessary renovations to the building. He remembers rolling his eyes, looking over at his mother, who was doing the same, and then whispering in his brother's ear something very close to, "They shouldn't discuss money here." He then remembers, just as some ass-hat from the balcony shouts down the number "two thousand," that his little brother, showing little hesitation, said loudly enough to be heard but not shouting, "Why don't we give it to the poor?"

I walked into the living room to find my mom sitting alone and looking at a photo album the way a woman who has one missing child would do. I sat down beside her on the couch. She looked up at me with a sort of what-are-you-about-to-say-to-me-that-I-don't-want-to-hear? look, and I began to speak.

"Why do you do this to yourself?" I asked.

"Because there's nothing else I can do," she answered quickly, as if she'd rehearsed it in her head.

"These are from last Christmas," I said, pointing to one of me standing in front of the Christmas tree.

"There aren't many of Gabe," she said plainly.

"He's camera shy," I said back.

"I remember when we snuck into his room and took that picture of him sleeping just so I'd have something besides your school picture to put on the fridge," she said, laughing.

"Yeah. He tried to convince me once that pictures steal part of your soul. He saw it on some documentary or something," I said.

"That's Gabe," she said, shaking her head, "always coming up with something bizarre to freak us out."

"It's been eight weeks, Mom," I said.

"It seems like so much longer, doesn't it?"

"Seems like eight years," I said quietly.

"We'll be buying school supplies soon," she said with a sigh.

I did not see Ada Taylor that day or the next one either. Instead I saw her car parked at the Quit Man's house and saw red when I closed my eyes. I saw Lucas Cader trying his best to make me laugh as we drove past. I saw Mena Prescott telling me I was better off. I saw my mom and dad watching TV in their bedroom, wearing their pajamas at three p.m. I saw Fulton Dumas mowing his front lawn slowly, headphones attached to his head, his hair in tall spikes, his eyes glazed over with boredom.

Lily's first annual Woodpecker Festival made me want to throw up in my mouth a little bit. I was only there because Lucas Cader had convinced me that it was a sure way of seeing Ada Taylor, who was becoming increasingly skilled at avoiding me and screening my phone calls. The festival took place where anything in Lily takes place: the city park. Let me give you a visual of this park. Two swing sets. One merry-go-round. Three slides, one metal and two plastic. One potentially danger-ous seesaw. A set of multicolored monkey bars. A ditch full of elephant ear plants and soggy grass. And best of all, a hexagonal gazebo with white latticework and a steeple. This park is where I first learned not to trust kids holding handfuls of dirt and not to jump from things when dared.

For the Woodpecker Festival, metal trailers had been brought in from as far as Harrison, and they now enclosed the park in a full circle. In the center, near the gazebo, a wooden fence separated the passersby from horses giving rides for five bucks each and a small petting zoo complete with goats, deer, and one black-and-white calf. To the left of the animals was a trailer that folded out into a stage, where, when Lucas and I arrived, a herd of glittery young girls clogged and tapped in unison to a song about honky-tonk, whatever the hell that is. On both sides of the stage hung long, narrow banners with crude likenesses of the Lazarus and the words LILY LOVES THE BIRD.

The one thing I did like about small-town festivals was the food. And more specifically, the corn dogs. There is a certain uniqueness to a festival corn dog, an undeniable combination of grease and cornmeal, of hunger built up from maneuvering around the crowd, of anticipation from the fifteen-minute line. Mustard? No thanks. I like my corn dogs bare and thrown nonchalantly into a paper sleeve. I like to see how fast it takes me to talk myself into a second or third one. As I was waiting in line for corn dog number two, a small boy ran by me with a stick horse between his legs, shouting, "Ride 'em, cowboy!" I laughed.

"When I was a kid, I made many a mile on stick horses," the man behind me said in my general direction.

"Is that right?" I asked, turning slightly around.

"Yep. Till I got a real one, and then it just wasn't the same," he said with a laugh, elbowing me in the shoulder.

I'd like to tell you that at that point I suddenly remembered a time when Gabriel came bouncing through the house on a stick horse, but that wouldn't be true. I did, however, imagine it happening anyway as I waited there, staring down at the little boy with sweat dripping from his temples as he raised one hand up into the air, let out intermittent yelps, and then trotted away.

"Makes you glad you don't have kids, huh?" the man behind me said.

"Yeah, I guess so," I said back.

"My grandson's about your age. What are you, fifteen or so?" he asked me.

"Seventeen," I said blankly.

"Oh. You look young. Lucky. Hold on to that. One day you'll appreciate it."

"I bet," I said before turning around to give my order.

Lucas Cader walked up to me as I sat on the steps of the gazebo, finishing corn dog number two and gazing over at the Baptist church choir performing on the stage. He sat down beside me, a burger in hand.

"These aren't so bad, really," he said.

"What?"

"Lazarus Burger," he said.

"Good Lord."

"Shut up. Festival's not so bad, is it?" Lucas asked.

"Not so good, either," I said.

"Well, have you seen her yet?" he asked.

"Ada? No. Have you?"

"No. But I saw Russell. He's over there, by the face-painting booth." Lucas pointed across the way to a small table surrounded by children that had been set up by my church.

The Quit Man sat in a wheelchair, connected to some sort of breathing machine. His face was swollen and bent to one side, his eyes larger than I remembered. His mother stood behind him, her hands grasping the handles of the chair and her head down close to his left ear. I watched as she pushed him down the narrow sidewalk and over to the petting zoo, where she parked him beside a bench and had a seat. The Quit Man no longer looked tough. He no longer looked mean. There was little to be intimidated by save for the pure amount of machinery enveloping his body. Just as Lucas was suggesting that we go check out the live snake exhibit, I saw Ada Taylor walk up to the Quit Man and give him a peck on the cheek. He smiled. I elbowed Lucas, who looked directly where I was looking.

"Shit," Lucas said.

"You got that right."

When one is watching the girl he thinks is his girlfriend whispering into the ear of her ex, he immediately imagines Russell Quitman suddenly yanking out the tubes from his neck, breaking free of his wheelchair, and lifting Ada Taylor off the ground in one quick swoop. He sees the Quit Man slowly plant a huge movie-star kiss on her lips and then put her down, laughing. His face goes from normal to zombie and back and forth. And behind them all the people cheer and clap and suddenly their faces too begin to shift and contort: Some drool, some develop sores, some hang their mouths open and begin to slide toward the laughing couple. And the boy with no brother stands alone in the center of the city gazebo, an army of zombies approaching. He turns to what he thinks is Lucas Cader to find none other than the Lazarus woodpecker seemingly floating beside him. He touches it to see if it's real and it bites his hand. Now bleeding, he watches the zombies move faster, Russell and Ada leading the pack. She, too, is now one of them, and in desperation, he looks over at the bird and whispers, "Can you find my brother?"

"It just looked like any other woodpecker to me," I said to my mom that evening in the kitchen.

"Yeah, but was it, like, huge?" she asked, stretching out her hands.

"It was big, but no big deal. I don't think, anyway."

"Lucas, what did you think?" she asked, dismissing my opinion.

"I thought it looked pretty amazing. It was a pretty good shot, too, right in the sky in between two trees, flying there like it had no clue it's the biggest mystery in Arkansas," he said excitedly.

"Dork," I said to him, kicking him under the table.

"Cullen, just because you think it's stupid doesn't mean we all have to," my mom said.

"I just think everyone's making a big deal out of something meaningless, that's all," I responded.

"It never hurts anyone to think life gives you second chances. God knows we need more of that around here lately," my mom said, tossing her dishrag onto the counter and walking out of the room.

Because Lucas had to go run some errands for his mom, I went out back and sat on the swing set that my dad had a friend weld together for us when I was six or so. It faced nothing but an open, grassy yard and a line of trees that began miles of woods filled with things making noises that used to keep me up all night. I began to whistle the song that Gabriel had jotted down on the folded piece of paper. I was known back then and still am for my remarkable ability to whistle any song I'd ever heard. I used to dream, when I was thirteen or so, that I'd hear about some national whistling contest and get to fly out to L.A. or something and win millions of dollars and be on the covers of magazines and have a trophy named after me.

As I sat there, I heard the *tap tap tap* of the Dumases' screen door and heard someone walking around the side of the house. I looked over to see John Barling, a cigarette in his mouth and a phone to his ear. He was standing near the back corner of the Dumas house when he began to shout into the phone.

"Damn it, Kathy, let me talk to my girls!"

He said something else that I couldn't make out before throwing the phone hard onto the ground and leaning his entire body against the side of the house. He stayed like this for a moment and then turned around and, crouching, began to reassemble the phone, whose battery had flown out. He looked up to see me swinging there. I did not try to hide the fact that I'd eavesdropped or that I was still watching his every move. He popped the battery back into the phone, flicked his cigarette to one side, and stood up. He began to walk toward me, his face emotionless.

"You mind?" he asked, pointing to the swing next to me.

"Go ahead," I said, unable to think of anything better.

He sat down on the swing and tightly grasped the chains on either side of him. He did one quick push and was then rocking back and forth. I was barely moving. He slowed down after a while, putting his feet down onto the ground again, and scratched the back of his head.

"My wife won't let me talk to my kids," he said.

"Oh," I replied.

"She says they don't wanna talk to me, but that just doesn't compute."

"How old are they?" I asked.

"Valerie's seven and Susanna's about to turn three," he said.

"How long's it been since you've seen 'em?" I asked.

"Too long. I try not to think about it too much. I'm a shitty father."

"Oh." This is what I say when I'm uncomfortable.

"Ya know, Cullen," he began, "your mind has a way of not letting you forget things you wish you could. Especially with people. Like, you'll always try your best to forget things that people say to you or about you, but you always remember. And you'll try to forget things you've seen that no one should see, but you just can't do it. And when you try to forget someone's face, you can't get it out of your head."

"I've been having trouble remembering my brother's face," I said to him.

"Is that right?" he asked.

"It's like when I try really hard to imagine him doing something or remember the last time I saw him, sometimes his face is just blank. And then other times I'll just be sitting in my room and all I see in my mind is Gabriel."

"That's the way it works, I guess," he said. "Your mind never lets you call the shots."

"Guess not," I said.

"I know there are people in this town who think I'm a bad man," he said, "but I could be worse."

"Yeah?" I asked.

"Yeah. I could be some traveling salesman, some con man taking everyone's money or something. I could be a murderer. All I want is to prove to the world that the Lazarus still exists. I know it does. I've seen it. I've heard it. It called me all the way down here from Oregon. This is my destiny." John Barling held one finger toward the sky, as if his "destiny" were floating just above it on display.

"I hope you're right," I said finally.

"What's your destiny, Cullen?" he asked, turning to face me and looking directly into my eyes. I shrugged.

"Well, do yourself a favor and don't start a family till you find it," he said, coughing.

With that said, John Barling got up, lit another cigarette, and began to slowly walk back toward the Dumas house. He turned around once to wink at me and then kept right along. I picked back up with my whistling, closed my eyes, and could see nothing but my brother's face.

Book Title #84: *One Million Miles on a Stick Horse.*

Chapter Sixteen
The Place Where Things Go Away

❧   Because life sometimes isn't all that predictable and because the human body is oftentimes the same way, Alma Ember and her husband Cabot Searcy did not have a baby as they'd planned. Instead they sat together on the floor of their small apartment's sparsely furnished living room and held hands, staring at the television and both secretly wondering what would happen next. In his eyes, Cabot Searcy had perhaps rushed into this marriage, but did not regret it for one single moment. Alma Ember was beginning to doubt every decision she'd ever made.

"This place is a dump," Alma said, standing up and walking toward the kitchen.

"Want some help?" Cabot asked, standing.

"Just stay outta my way, please," she said, spraying the counter with orange liquid.

"Okay," he said, sitting down on the couch and picking up the remote.

Beverly Ember had given up in those few weeks trying to be directly involved in her granddaughter's life, questioning whether or not she had been overbearing or too nosy. She did, however, still hand Alma a check nearly every week, trusting that she would use it for food or rent. Alma would say thanks, would show a slight expression of guilt, and would kiss her grandmother on the cheek. Cabot Searcy had lost favor with his uncle Jeff when he impregnated Alma, leading to his being cut off completely. Now Cabot spent his days not looking for jobs, but pretending to as Alma served complicated coffees in various Italian-named sizes down the street.

Four months after Cabot found work as a satellite TV salesman, Alma Ember decided to move back in with her grandmother. Beverly was quite happy. Alma was somewhat relieved, but still sad. Cabot Searcy lost his job, would not get out of bed, and called Alma Ember fifty-seven times over the span of three days. This became his life. In between placing phone calls and writing long-drawn-out, pathetic, and often incoherent letters, Cabot continued his study of the very subject that had, unbeknownst to him, driven Alma away: the potential of humankind. Still reading from ancient texts, secret writings,

and the Bible his mother had given him at age fourteen, Cabot
had taken his curiosity to obsession. He stayed up most nights
reading, copying interesting scriptures or writing his theories
down in a book very similar to the one carried by Benton Sage.
He had told Alma the day before she left that had God not killed
the Grigori angels so many years ago, their baby would have
lived. Alma cried silently in bed that night before tiptoeing
into the bathroom and sitting on the edge of the tub with her
head hung between her knees. She watched a few tears crash
onto the gray linoleum floor. She wiped them away with her
foot, then stood up and stared into the mirror. Splashing her
face and looking up, Alma Ember focused to see if she could
distinguish between the teardrops and water. Her eyes red. Her
hair several days unwashed. Her hand tightly gripping the side
of the sink.

This had not been the first time Cabot had blamed God for
the loss of his child. In fact, he had begun to write down lists of
all the world's evils, as if he were building up an army of words
to fight some heavenly battle. He had taken Benton's notes and
not blown them out of proportion so much as he had strapped
an atom bomb to every letter of every word. Alma knew this,
and so she left. She had little faith that he would realize how his
own mind was deceiving him.

He was, in a sense, seeking to prove that the very creator of
mankind was also its greatest oppressor. It all gave Alma a headache, and as his religious ramblings began to grow more frequent
and nonsensical, Alma began to fear her once charming, seemingly normal husband.

CHAPTER SEVENTEEN
This May Be the End of the World

❧   It was at some point in mid-July that my father began asking me about college. I'll tell you this much: College was the last thing I cared about the summer that my brother disappeared and that Ada Taylor started sleeping with me. But my father suddenly seemed so preoccupied with it, hassling me to look at catalogs he'd sent for and to visit this website or that to get an idea of some campus halfway across the country that I had never heard of before. He suddenly wanted to know what my interests were. What I wanted to major in. What my dreams for my life were, and how I planned on making them come true. What impact I wanted to have on the world. To tell you the truth, it really all sort of pissed me off at first. There

I was, seventeen years old, and the first time my dad showed me the littlest bit of attention was when I least wanted him to. Didn't he know that all I felt like doing was fading into the background? Leaning against a wall and disappearing into it? Lying on the couch, hoping the cushions would swallow me up?

And even worse, he had my mom trying to get information out of me, asking random questions like, "Do you think you're more right brained or more left brained?" and "If you had to pick between living on the East Coast or the West Coast, which would you choose?" I never told her what I wanted to give as my answer, that I would choose whichever coast my brother happened to be hiding on or locked in a basement near or buried under. I never told her that even if I did know what I wanted to be, I still couldn't bear the thought of leaving Lily as long as I knew my brother might show up one day or that whoever was responsible for his leaving was still out there somewhere waiting to do it again and again and again until a thousand Cullen Witters were seeing zombies of their dead brothers standing by their beds at night. I would need to be there when he showed back up. I would need to be there to protect him. I didn't give a shit about college, and I was tired of being made to think about it constantly. So I left the house one day and went to Ada Taylor's house, and she wasn't there. So I went to Lucas Cader's, and he was sitting on the front steps outside. I sat down beside him. He could tell I was angry because he didn't say anything. This is what Lucas knew to do when I was mad.

"She's at his house again," I said to him.

"Damn," he said.

"That guy's more appealing in a wheelchair than I am able-bodied. How sad is that?"

"It's got nothing to do with you," Lucas said.

"Sure feels that way," I said back.

The next morning, as we sat in my kitchen, I promised Lucas we wouldn't talk about the Ada situation. My mom, who had stayed over at Aunt Julia's for three nights in a row, walked into the kitchen, set her bag down on the counter, turned to look at Lucas and me at the table, and said, "That's it for me. Julia can take care of herself from now on," and walked out of the room. Lucas grinned and shoveled another bite of waffle into his mouth. I got up and walked down the hall and into my mom's room. She was sitting on the edge of her bed. She was not crying. She was not laughing. She did and said nothing.

"What happened?" I asked in that I-hope-it's-okay-if-I-talk-right-now kind of way.

"We were talking about Oslo and how he was so cute when he was a baby," she said.

"Wasn't he on a billboard or something?" I asked.

"Yeah. They put him up on the hospital billboard when he was a few weeks old."

"Yeah," I said.

"Anyway, we were talking about that when she started saying something about heaven."

"Heaven?" I asked.

"Yeah. She said something like she hoped that when we got to heaven we were all babies again."

"Cool," I said.

"And then"—my mother began to tear up—"she said that all she could do anymore was think about Oslo and Gabriel up there as babies, crawling around on a solid white floor together."

Just as it had my mom, the thought of Gabriel not being on Earth anymore, and also of Oslo in heaven, started to upset me as I walked outside to take the trash out. I wondered if Oslo had, in fact, made it up there. I wondered whether or not mercy was given to someone who so continually screwed everything up. Then I wondered what made me different from him, besides the fact that I wasn't a junkie. I had no real future to speak of. No goals. No aspirations. No desire to do anything but wait around for something big to happen, something miraculous to occur. Maybe Oslo had felt the same way, like what was the point of giving up these drugs that made him feel good when all he was doing here was waiting around for the good to start? But he was wrong. Was I wrong too? To be waiting around on the impossible? And was Aunt Julia right? Would we all turn back into babies when we died? If that's how we started out, didn't it make sense to think that we'd go back to that original form? That we'd be completely innocent again? That we'd know nothing of sadness or loneliness or boredom?

"You think too much," Lucas said to me on the banks of the White River the next day.

"*I* think too much?" I asked, my voice raised.

"Yeah. You can't just sit back and relax without analyzing every little thing," he said.

"That's what you do, Lucas!" I said.

"Only sometimes," he said back.

"Just as much as I do, I'd say."

"Whatever. That's not the point. The point is, you—sorry, *we* need to learn how to just calm down and take everything in before trying to pick it all apart."

"Why?" I asked.

"Because we always end up ruinin' it before it begins."

It was the nine-week mark when my mother stopped doing things. Things like buying bread and milk. Things like showering or brushing her teeth. Things like answering the phone sitting right next to her. She hadn't been to the salon in four days, and so my dad found her appointment book and called all her regular customers to indefinitely postpone their appointments. I was sitting in my room the day that she started throwing canned goods and cereal boxes across the kitchen and into the wall. The first thing my dad shouted was, "Cullen, stay back there!" I was in the living room when she decided to start cussing out late-night television reruns, telling Ted Danson to kiss her ass and Mary Tyler Moore to go do something quite crude to herself.

My dad remained patient. He calmed her down. He watched her from all angles of the room. He brought her glasses of water with tiny blue pills. He looked at me the way one looks at you in a funeral home. The way you would look at someone who had just been given bad news. Still he remained consistent with his goal of finding me a college, talking over my mom's sobs or shouts to tell me about some new school he'd read about in a magazine or some career that seemed to be headed in the right direction. I found it exhausting to listen to, but I didn't quite have the heart to dismiss him altogether. He was trying, and I had no right not to let him.

"If I went to U of A, would they let me room with Lucas?" I asked my dad.

"Not sure, but I think you can request to do that or something," he said.

"Yeah. Maybe I should call up there and ask," I said, causing my dad's face to light up like I'd seen only a few times before.

"Hey," he said to me as I walked out of the room, "be sure to ask them about their honors program, too. I bet you anything you're eligible."

I did not call U of A when I left the room. Instead I walked past the telephone, past the kitchen, down the hall, and into my bedroom, where Lucas Cader was asleep on the floor. I stepped over him and got into my bed. I pulled out my journal and opened it to the first blank page. I wrote down the conversation I'd just had with my dad, and then I closed the book and put it back under my mattress. Closing my eyes, I began to imagine walking around a large, crowded college campus. Everyone around me was smiling, introducing themselves to friends of friends, talking about the big game last night, wearing their newly purchased red and white sweatshirts. And I was right in the middle, everyone moving quickly around me, noises flooding my brain, not moving a muscle. My face was expressionless as the world spun around me as if I were the sun.

When I woke up, Lucas was doing jumping jacks in the

middle of my bedroom. I sat up, looked at him, and waited for him to notice that I'd awakened. When he did, he simply looked down at me, smiled, and continued to jump up and down, flailing his arms and legs out with each hop.

"What the hell are you doing?" I asked him.

"Getting my endorphins kicked in," he said.

"Why?"

"'Cause we're running the Woodpecker Relay tonight," he said.

"The what?" I asked.

"The Woodpecker Relay, Cullen. Do you live under a rock?"

"I try to, yes," I said.

"I signed you and me and Mena up to run in the race. It starts at four thirty, so you better get changed."

"No. I'm not running in a stupid race!" I shouted.

"Cullen, I signed you up. You have to."

"No, I don't."

"Come on. You know you'll end up having fun and thank me later," he said, still jumping into the air.

"No I won't, because I'm *not* going!" I said, walking out of the room.

Lucas followed behind me down the hallway, his breathing heavy. I opened up the refrigerator to find it empty, and when I closed it, Lucas was standing on the other side of the door. He had that waiting-for-me-to-give-in-to-his-odd-request-and-just-go-with-the-flow sort of look on his face. I turned around and took a seat at the dining table. He sat down across from me, his breathing still heavy. He put both his elbows up on the table and leaned down to look directly at my face. He nodded his head slightly. His look was all confidence.

"Hell no," I said.

"Cullen, don't be crazy."

"Lucas, just go to your damn relay and leave me the hell alone!" I shouted, standing up and walking into the living room, where my dad sat flipping through the channels.

"Mr. Sam, tell him that runnin' the relay'll be fun," Lucas said to my dad.

"Cullen, the relay will be fun," my dad said robotically.

"See, he wants you to do it. So let's go."

With that I stood up, my face only about two inches from Lucas Cader's, and said the following in my lowest of voices:

"Lucas, I understand that you want to have fun. That you like to distract yourself from life by going and doing these ridiculous things and laughing the whole time while you do them. I know you want to pretend that everything's okay by trying your best to act normal, but I don't. I want to sit in this house and mope around and be sad and revel in the fact that my life is complete shit from here on out. So go get your girlfriend, go run your race, get the hell out of my house, and don't come back until you're ready to start acting like you didn't forget that my little brother and your friend is still out there somewhere having God knows what done to him by God knows who."

Lucas Cader walked quickly out the front door and my dad turned the television off, stood up, and left me in the middle of the living room. I dragged my feet all the way back to my bedroom and threw myself face-first onto my bed. I felt the hot air of my breath on my face. I smelled the cotton of my sheets. And I screamed just loud enough for the sound to be muffled, as if it hadn't existed at all.

Dr. Webb says that losing a sibling is oftentimes much harder for a person than losing any other member of the family. "A sibling represents a person's past, present, and future," he says. "Spouses have each other, and even when one eventually dies, they have memories of a time when they existed before that other person and can more readily imagine a life without them. Likewise, parents may have other children to be concerned with—a future to protect for them. To lose a sibling is to lose the one person with whom one shares a lifelong bond that is meant to continue on into the future." I understood this to mean that as a seventeen-year-old whose brother was most likely dead, I was acting like a complete ass-hat for a good reason. Not only had my brother disappeared, but—and bear with me here—a part of my very being had gone with him. Stories about us could, from then on, be told from only one perspective. Memories could be told but not shared.

Ten weeks to the day was all it took for my mom to officially move into Gabriel's bedroom. The door stayed closed most of the time, and my dad and I stopped trying to get her to answer. She did eat about once a day, though, so at least we found comfort in the fact that she had some will to live. If, as Dr. Webb says, there are several stages to the grieving process, my mom was smack-dab in the middle of the bat-shit insane stage, barely able to speak without stammering, unable to sleep for more than an hour or so, obsessed with reading Gabriel's collection of books and listening to his CDs. The day after she took over his room, she opened the door and pulled me in as I walked down the hallway. She sat me down on the bed. She was wearing pink-and-white-striped pajamas and no makeup.

"I want you to hear this song, Cullen. It's amazing."

She pressed play on his small stereo, and I waited to hear something. Nothing happened.

"Shit," she said, sitting down Indian-style on the floor in front of the stereo.

"Here, Mom, let me—"

"No, stop. I can do this," she interrupted, pressing two more buttons while half sticking out her tongue.

What played was the middle of a song I'd never heard before, and I closed my eyes, listening to every word.

> *Staring at the sun*
> *Oh my own voice cannot save me now*
> *Standing in the sea*
> *It's just one more breath and then down I go.*

I looked at my mom, who moved her lips to the words, and I wondered how many times she'd sat there and listened to it that day. She swayed back and forth, her eyes looking up to the ceiling, one hand moving by her side, seeming to slowly swat away invisible flies. When the song ended, my mom pressed the stop button, let her arms fall to her sides, and looked at me as if I was supposed to say something.

"I liked it," I said.

"I knew you would," she said.

"Where does he find this stuff?" I asked her.

"I don't know, but I love it," she said, now rubbing one hand on the carpet.

"Are you gonna come outta here anytime soon?" I asked her.

"You really do look just like him, ya know?" she asked me, staring at my face.

"Mom, please," I said.

"You do. When you were about six and five, people used to ask me if you were twins. You looked like twins."

"You wanna go get some food or something?" I asked her, standing up.

"I want you to know that it's gonna be okay, Cullen."

"Mom."

"School'll start soon, and one day you're gonna come home and Gabe's gonna be sittin' right here on the floor listening to this song."

Ada Taylor agreed to meet me at the only coffee shop in town, which also doubled as a bookstore. We sat across from each other and awkwardly waited for the other to speak. Ada had a look on her face to suggest that she felt terribly bad about something. I felt as if I had the same look on my own face as I sipped my coffee and finally spoke.

"Ada, I'm a little confused," I said.

"I know you are," she said back.

"About what's going on between you and Russell."

"Right," she said.

"And about you suddenly not returning my phone calls and never being home."

She stared at me as if she either had nothing to say or no way to say it.

"Do you have anything at all to say here?" I asked.

"I need to take care of Russell. He needs me. I owe it to him," she said.

"What does that mean? You owe it to him? *You* didn't break his neck!" I started talking too loudly.

"It means that had Russell never met me, he probably would never have ended up down there in Florida drunk off his ass and wrecking his car. It's my fault, any way you slice it. I never got a chance to take care of the last two, so I need to be there for him now."

"And what about me, then?" I asked.

"What about you, Cullen?" she asked, sounding frustrated.

I waited in silence for her to apologize.

"Cullen, you're just in love with the idea of us being together and the idea of this working. It's not me, I promise."

"It's not you," I repeated back, a blank look on my face.

"I'm sorry, Cullen. I really am. I know this sucks. But you're better off anyway. And you'll be fine. You needed me. Now someone else needs me."

As she walked out the door, I took a sip of my coffee and

stared over at the couple sitting to my right. They were looking at me in that we-just-heard-you-get-dumped sort of way, so I raised my coffee cup in their direction, as if to say "cheers," and took another sip. I threw a dollar down on the table and walked out the door.

Lucas Cader came back three days after I'd asked him to leave. He hadn't run in the relay, and the left side of his jaw was purple and swollen. He sat down beside me on the couch, nodded hello to my dad in the recliner beside him, and stared at the TV. My dad turned up the volume to block out the music coming from my brother's room and, leaning up just enough to make eye contact with me, pointed to his jaw and then to Lucas.

"What happened?" I asked, a grin on my face.

"Nothing," he said.

"No, really, what the hell happened to your face?"

"I said nothing. Just leave it alone," he answered.

"Fine. Just walk into a person's living room with a bruised-up face and give no one any explanation for it," I said.

"Okay, I'll tell you," he said. My dad muted the television and sat up. Lucas cracked the smile of someone with only half a working face.

"So, I left here the other day after you told me to—"

"Sorry," I interrupted.

"It's fine. Anyway, I left here and went to pick up Mena. She was running late, so by the time we got to the park, all the runners were lined up and John Barling, of all people, was standing on the stage and holding a pistol in the air. He welcomed everyone and began to count. And at that very moment, when Mena took off for the runners' line, I took off for the stage. I ran up the steps and ran across to Barling and then I just socked him right in the nose."

"You did what?" I asked.

"Damn," my dad said.

"I socked him hard, too, but he's stronger than I thought, and before I could do anything else he swung and caught my mouth. That's why I look like this."

"Damn," I said.

"Still hurts like a bitch too." Lucas laughed.

"Why'd you do it?"

"To show you I haven't forgotten what's important, I guess," he mumbled.

"Hell, Lucas, you could've just said so," I replied.

The next morning I woke up before Lucas and tiptoed my way out of the room. I poured myself a bowl of cereal, Fruity Pebbles, because that's what I had for about every meal that summer, which caused the roof of my mouth to be constantly coated in a sugary film. I sat down across from my dad at the table; he was slowly stirring his coffee and staring down at a crossword puzzle.

"I called the Office of Student Housing," my dad said, never looking up.

"Yeah?" I asked.

"Yeah. They said you just have to fill out some form and

Lucas has to do the same and you guys will have yourselves a dorm room."

"Thanks, Dad," I said.

Gabriel and I used to play this game we liked to call What If? where the object was to take turns creating the most absurd "what if?" scenarios. We had played a particularly good round of this game as we lay on the roof of our house just a couple of weeks before he went missing. Our original reason for lying on the roof was to view a widely publicized meteor shower. Gabriel wouldn't let himself miss one of these, no matter the hour of night, as they only happened once every few years.

"What if humans began to evolve and sprout wings?" he said, never breaking his stare at the dark sky.

"What if I already have them and have been hiding them all these years?" I said back.

"What if I throw you off this roof for being a liar?" he said with a laugh.

"What if I used my secret wings to fly away?" I laughed back.

"What if nonwinged humans started hunting winged humans for sport?" Gabriel asked.

"That would definitely happen in Lily," I added.

"What if we drafted up some laws in anticipation of this evolutionary event?" Gabriel suggested.

"What if we called them 'It's Not Easy Being Winged: Rules and Guidelines for the Recently Able to Fly'?"

"Perfect." Gabriel sighed.

In those days when it felt as if summer was dwindling away and my future refused to stop beckoning and harassing me at every turn, I started to find comfort in my own little game of What If? Most of these scenarios, naturally, centered on my brother. "What if," I would ask myself while driving down the road or sitting on the couch or trying to fall asleep, "what if Gabriel were like the Lazarus woodpecker, and he popped up one day as if nothing had ever happened to him? What if this was all real—this stupid woodpecker thing? What if things really did come back to life in this awful place?" This always made me think about the time Gabriel told me why he would always have faith in mankind. He said:

"Cullen, people can't give up on other people yet. We all get a second chance, you know? We get to start over like Noah after the flood. No matter how evil man gets, he always gets a second chance one way or another."

Book Title #85: *God Knows What.*

When one is lying on the floor of his bedroom exactly ten weeks and three days after his brother has vanished off the face of the Earth, he begins to imagine quite a grandiose scene. The doorbell rings and his mother, in a black dress, opens it up to greet his aunt Julia and her husband, the doctor James Fouke, by her side. He doesn't look dead at all, Cullen Witter thinks to himself, getting up from the floor and moving to the couch. The doorbell rings again as Julia and James move into the kitchen. He jumps up and beats his mother to the door, opening it to find a nicely groomed Lucas Cader, necktie and all, with Mena Prescott attached to his right arm. She is wearing a black dress as well, only hers has no straps and is much tighter fitting. He silently motions them to go into the living room, and as soon as he tries to shut the door, he sees someone else approaching. He waits there, holding the door open, until Ada Taylor walks through, kisses his cheek, and continues on into the house. He shuts the door, shaking his head with a smile, and walks slowly into the kitchen where he finds his parents, aunt, and uncle all raising champagne glasses into the air. *Clink.*

He walks into the living room but turns around as soon as the doorbell rings once again. The door opens before he can get to it and Oslo Fouke steps in, smiling, in a white button-down shirt and black necktie. He smirks at his cousin, looks him up and down, and shakes his outstretched hand. Oslo steps to one side and walks into the living room, where he takes a seat beside Lucas and Mena on the couch. He asks Lucas about school. He comments on Mena's dress. He does not look dead either as he asks Ada Taylor to dance and they begin to sway in the center of the room. From behind them, Cullen Witter sees someone walk down the hall. He tries to stand up on his tiptoes to see over his guests and as he does, Gabriel Witter comes walking into the room from the opposite side, turns his eyebrows up at his cousin, and walks right past Cullen, lightly patting his shoulder. He sees Gabriel's mouth moving, but no sound comes out. He notices the same thing when anyone else tries to speak in his direction.

Alma Ember and her mother barge into the house with an odd

familiarity and go directly into the dining room, where Cullen believes he hears the faintest sounds of laughter. He steps into the room, and instead of finding a four-chaired wooden table bought on sale at Lily's only furniture store, he sees a long table with eight chairs on each side and one on each end. The table is covered in a white lace cloth and dotted by silver platters with lids, bowls of grapes, baskets of bread, and glasses of bubbling liquids. His parents are seated at either end of the table, and his aunt and uncle are right next to his mom on the left side. Alma and her mother take a seat next to them, and as Cullen tries to leave the room, his friends pour through the doorway and take their seats.

Just as Cullen surveys the room for a seat of his own, Russell Quitman stands before him, his friend Neil at his heels, and extends a hand. Cullen shakes it, noting this to be the first time, and motions them toward the table, staring down at Russell's working legs as the two walk away. Neil turns back to wink at Cullen and makes an I'm-shooting-an-imaginary-yet-playful-gun-at-you hand gesture his way. Cullen stays by the door and waits only a few seconds before hearing someone else walking up the porch steps. John Barling, Shirley Dumas, and Fulton all file into the house and greet Cullen with handshakes and smiles. They make their way into the dining room as Cullen looks at them in confusion and shakes his head. He leaves the door open now and retreats to the dining room with all the others.

He takes a seat to the left of his father, who is saying something that Cullen cannot hear. He tries intently to read his father's lips but can't seem to pick up on what he is saying.

Bored with this, he reaches across the table to take the lid off a huge silver platter. Just as he does so, a hand slaps his away. It is Shirley Dumas, who smiles at him and shakes her head as if to say, *It's not time yet, young man.* He smiles, picking up his glass to take a sip of whatever has been poured into it. He tastes nothing, though, and puts it back down. He looks across the table and beside him and down at the opposite end. Everyone is smiling. Talking. Laughing. He feels hands placed on his shoulders and turns to find Gabriel, standing there with a guitar strapped around his neck and arm. Gabriel smiles down at Cullen and walks over to their mom's end of the table. He pulls out the empty chair to her left and stands up on it, beginning to tune his guitar. Cullen looks around; everyone has stopped talking. Their smiles remain.

His brother begins to strum the guitar with what looks like skill but sounds to Cullen like nothing but silence. He wonders when his brother got back and when he learned to play guitar. He sits back in his seat, though, and watches intently as everyone begins to move slowly to whatever song Gabriel is playing. He looks up to see Gabriel's lips moving. He is singing now. His eyes are closed. He is really killing this silent song, Cullen thinks. He watches the guests watching his brother, Mena resting her head on Lucas's shoulder, Oslo holding a cigarette lighter in the air, his mom wiping happy tears from her eyes. And then he sees something out of the corner of his own eye. It is red, black, and white, and it is fast. He looks up at Gabriel, still strumming, still singing, and he sees resting on his shoulder a two-foot-tall Lazarus woodpecker. He looks around to find that no one seems to be concerned with it. He looks directly at John Barling and tries to call out to him, but no words leave his lips. John Barling sits in silence, a big dumb smile on his bristly face, with Shirley Dumas swaying beside him. The doorbell rings. Cullen jumps up, runs through the kitchen, and sees Vilonia Kline standing behind the screen door. He motions her in. She shoots him a smile. She walks in front of him and takes a seat, waving to everyone at the table but then looking up to admire Gabriel's performance.

Cullen stands in the back corner of the room. He examines the faces of his friends, his family, of people he barely knows and people he can't stand the sight of. He leans his back against the wall. He still hears nothing. He tries to scream "HELLO!" but nothing comes out once again. His father looks back at him and motions for him to sit down. He does. He watches his brother with everyone else. He wishes he could hear the song. He wishes he could hear his brother's voice one more time. He looks at the bird. It looks back at him and flaps its wings one dramatic time. Its beady eyes are fixed on his. It opens its mouth, perhaps making a sound, but maybe not. Cullen can't tell. He cringes at the closeness of the bird's large bill to his brother's neck, wishing it would fly away. It doesn't. It stays there and begins moving its head up and down as if dancing in its own way to the silent song. Cullen looks across the table at Neil and then over at Russell, whose jaw is beginning to droop strangely. He motions to Russell, pointing to his own jaw, but Russell waves his motion away and points up to Gabriel. He looks over at Oslo and sees the same thing happening to his jaw. His eyes also begin to droop. His face becomes completely contorted. He looks back at Russell; his eyes are doing this as well. Cullen stands up, backs away from the table, and realizes that everyone around him is beginning to look very strange. His back bumps into the wall, and he lowers himself to the floor. The people in front of him become zombies, moving slowly, standing up, all leaning to one side or the other, eyes hung low, mouths open, and swinging dead-like. They all stand in place, still focused on Gabriel, who remains normal, still strumming, still singing. He looks down at Cullen. And though his lips are still moving, he appears to be frightened. Cullen looks to Lucas Cader but finds a zombie in his place. He stands up and reaches for his brother. Gabriel does not move. Cullen shakes his little brother's shoulder, and the guitar falls to one side. The bird flies off across the room and lands on Oslo's head. Gabriel looks at him blankly, his face still human, his eyes still frightened, and he mouths Cullen's name before crashing headfirst onto the table. Cullen backs away again, tries to make his way to the door, but runs into something. He turns around and sees his house full of these same unhuman beings. They all walk toward him, their arms outstretched, their heads bobbing, their feet dragging. He climbs up on the table and tries to lift Gabriel's head. He suddenly finds nothing in his hands but empty clothes. He begins to scream and nothing comes out. He does it again. Still nothing. He closes his eyes. He clenches his fists. He opens his mouth as wide as it will go and lets out the loudest sound he's ever made. He opens his eyes to find himself sitting on the table in an empty room. He counts the chairs; there are four on each side. He hops down, shakes his head, and straightens his hair with one hand. He walks into the kitchen and sits down beside his brother at the breakfast table. His brother looks over at him and says, in a whisper, "This is how it ends."

Book Title #86: *Zombie Dinner Party*.

Chapter Eighteen
You Couldn't Find a Nicer Guy If You Tried

🐾 It was hard for Alma to surrender to the fact that returning to Lily was probably in her best interest. She was no longer in college, having dropped out during her third semester because of morning sickness, two Ds, and one F. Lily, she thought, would be simpler than Savannah. More familiar. More supportive. And most important, Lily would have less Cabot Searcy. Since she'd left him, Cabot had continued harassing her, calling late at night, showing up with flowers or candy or big stuffed bears, sending messages to her through friends and acquaintances. His efforts had proven unsuccessful, and this became quite evident when he was served divorce papers by a short, stocky man named something like Carl or Joe.

Beverly paid for Alma's flight home. She hugged her tightly. She cried. She whispered into her only granddaughter's ear, "You are so loved." Alma boarded the second flight of her life and within two hours she was back in Arkansas, standing near baggage claim and waiting to see her mother appear on the escalator. When she did, everything was good and nobody was sad. The crowd moved around them, people running into one another, mothers trying to keep up with their children, husbands telling their wives to hurry up, luggage wheels rolling and squeaking, an electronic voice announcing a delayed flight.

Cabot Searcy had talked to his wife only once since she'd moved back to Arkansas, and just long enough for her to beg him once again to sign the papers so she could get on with her life. In response to his endless questions as to why she'd left him, Alma hung up the phone. This was the same day that Cabot Searcy fell asleep and saw what he called a heavenly vision. He stood alone in a treeless field, nothing but stumps and dead limbs scattered around him. From above his head a beam of slightly green light set his body aglow. He heard a voice and saw himself look up into the sky. When he woke up, he repeated what little he could remember, a verse from Hebrews about Enoch: "Taken up so he should not see death; and he was not found."

"What's it matter if they find that bird or not?" Alma Ember asked her mother some weeks later.

"Well, sweetie, something like this could cause a lot of business and such to come to town. Lily could use all the people it can get, ya know?" her mother replied.

"Guess so." Alma shrugged.

"Plus, isn't it excitin' to think that something can just come back like that?"

"So it's just been hiding here for all these years?" Alma asked.

"Yeah," her mom said back.

"Seems like it didn't wanna be found," Alma said, filing her fingernails.

That night in bed, Alma Ember thought about how similar she and the Lazarus woodpecker were. They both left. They both came back. They both wanted to be as invisible as possible. She imagined herself sitting by the river and watching hundreds of birds fly all around and above her. She laughed at the thought of being there, seeing that amazing thing that was giving everyone in town so much hope. She decided then that if ever she were to catch a glimpse of the bird, she would tell no one. She would simply smile, nod her head, and continue on with whatever she was doing, knowing that she had saved the bird in some small way.

It was by chance that Alma ran into an old friend from church at the grocery store one day. He asked her how she was, told her she looked great, and with all the confidence in the world asked her if the rumors were true about her getting married. She hid nothing, laughing through the entire conversation, and said little about Cabot save for mentioning that he had gone "a little bit crazy." This encounter was the first time since she'd moved back that Alma felt unjudged. The first time she'd been able to talk about it without feeling stupid. And all of this with some high schooler she hadn't seen since she graduated. Yes, Lucas Cader had made her day. And though their conversation had ended minutes before, Lucas approached her once more in the parking lot and asked her a surprising question.

"You know Cullen Witter, right?" he asked.

"Yeah, what's he up to?"

"Well, here's the thing. Cullen's a great guy, my best friend in the whole world. Couldn't find a nicer guy if you tried. So I was thinking, since you're suddenly back in town and all, you might want to come out with us tonight."

"With you and Cullen?" Alma asked, confusion on her face.

"No, no. Me, Cullen, and Mena."

"Mena Prescott?" she asked.

"Yeah. We've been dating for a while."

"Oh. That's good, Lucas. She's so pretty," she said.

"So it's a date, then? Tonight?" Lucas asked.

"Umm, are you sure?" Alma asked.

"It's just a movie with some friends. You know this town is boring you to death already," Lucas joked.

"You're right. I'm in."

"Pick you up about six fifty, the show starts at seven fifteen," Lucas said, walking away in reverse.

"I'll be ready."

"See ya."

"Bye, Lucas, thanks."

Cabot Searcy had never been to Arkansas before the day he landed at the Little Rock airport. He had also never rented a car before stepping into the dark green Ford Taurus and taking the entrance ramp onto the interstate. Terrible at directions, Cabot was relieved that he had only to travel this one road in order to eventually stumble on Lily, Arkansas, where he hoped to find and patch things up with his runaway wife. He listened to the radio loudly as he passed exit after exit, casually noting the number on each glowing sign as he sang along and snapped his fingers wildly. This time he would sit her down, hold her hand, and cry if he had to. He would apologize for his behavior. Promise a new start. Ensure her a perfect life.

After getting off the interstate, he drove some ten or fifteen miles before coming upon a wooden sign illuminated only by a single spotlight secured to the ground below it. The sign read in big, bold red letters: WELCOME TO LILY! and underneath it had been added, in slightly smaller letters of black and green, HOME OF THE LAZARUS WOODPECKER!

"I'll be damned," Cabot said to himself, turning the radio off.

He had told Alma the night before on the phone that he would sign the papers and mail them to her attorney in Savannah. He had lied, of course, and had instead gone straight to his uncle to beg for enough cash to buy a plane ticket. After passing through the dismal, dimly lit town, Cabot pulled up to a small motel with several of its sign's neon letters burnt out. He had just enough for one night, and turning the key to room 16, he glanced over to his right to see, leaning against the side of the building, a large, new sign reading, in unlit neon letters, THE LAZARUS MOTEL.

Waking up with his Bible beside him, Cabot stuck a finger into his left eye to adjust his contact, stood up, and then knelt down on the floor, placing his elbows onto the bed. He silently asked God to provide him with the answers he so desperately searched for. Why wouldn't Alma come back to him? What was the point of his finding Benton Sage's journal? Why had he ended up in Lily, Arkansas? He coughed. He said amen. He walked into the bathroom and took a shower.

It was around noon when Cabot found Alma's house, and only knew it to be so from her maiden name stuck to the mailbox in tiny black and gold letters. For curiosity's sake, he opened up the mailbox, rifled through the envelopes, and threw them back in. There were no cars home. He walked into the carport and tried his best to peer through the high window of the side door. He saw nothing but a darkened kitchen. As he turned to walk away and back to his car, he heard the door behind him open. He turned around to see Alma's mother standing there with the screen door still shut in front of her.

"What do you want?" she asked.

"Ma'am, I'm Cabot. I'm Alma's husband," he said, walking closer.

"I know who you are. Why'd you come here?"

"I wanna see Alma. Is she here?" he asked, still walking forward.

"Stay where you are, okay? She's not home."

"Can I wait for her then?" he asked.

"No. That's not a good idea. Do you have the papers?" she asked him, opening the screen door up just enough to let her hand through, her palm facing upward.

"I mailed them yesterday. To the lawyer," he said.

"Good. Then why don't you go on back home now? She'll be gone for a while. She told me y'all were through. Now, I'm sorry. But that's that."

"Ma'am, let me in. Please."

"Cabot Searcy, you turn around and get back in your car and get outta here," she said, closing the screen door back.

"I have to see her," he said. "I need to. Just to say good-bye."

"You'll wait in the car then, across the street. And don't you walk back over here unless I say so. You got it?"

"Yes, ma'am. Thanks," he said, walking toward the car, where he would wait for thirty-seven minutes, each one counted intently by Alma's mother.

Alma Ember rounded the corner in her mother's maroon Honda and pulled into the driveway. She got out, looked across the street, and saw her husband staring at her from a green car. She stood there, waiting for him to walk over, but he did not move. Her mother opened the door and shouted, "Alma, I told him to stay over there until it was okay!" Alma looked back at her mother, held a finger up as if to say *Give me one minute*, and began to walk across the street. Cabot had already rolled the passenger window down when she approached the car and rested one hand against the door. She leaned down and looked in at him. He had been crying.

"Cabot, what the hell?"

"Alma, I know we can fix this. I know it," he said, reaching for the door handle.

"Stay in the car, Cabot," she said.

"I just . . . I'm so glad to see you. You look so good and I just—"

"You need to go home now. You need to go home and mail those papers and you need to stop all this."

"Alma, I love you," he said, leaning over to get closer.

"Cabot, it's done. I've got things to do. I've got to get ready to go somewhere. I have a life here. I think you should go back to yours in Georgia."

As she walked away, Alma began to think of all the things she hadn't said to him that she should have. She should have told him to see a therapist. She should have told him that he was a kind, good guy who just couldn't seem to hold himself together right. She should have told him that she had moved on, had been dating someone, had gotten over him completely. She should have lied through her teeth to ensure that he would get the point. And so, she turned back around to see Cabot still sitting there, his hands gripping the steering wheel, his head leaned down. She walked back up to the window, stuck her head inside, and said this:

"Cabot, you weren't the worst husband in the world. It was good. A lot of it was good. But I knew it was over and so I just had to go. I'm sorry. That's the way it happened and there's no way to fix it. So I'm gonna go in and get ready for my date and you're gonna drive back to Little Rock, get on a plane, and go home. Okay?"

"You have a date?" he asked.

"Yes."

"With who?" he asked.

"Cabot, you don't know anybody here. What's it matter?"

"At least tell me his name and I'll go. I promise. I'll go."

"His name's Cullen. He's nice. You'd like him. Please leave."

With that, Cabot Searcy started up his rented car and soon disappeared from Alma's view. That would be the last time Alma Ember ever saw her husband. Rounding a curve, Cabot Searcy began to think about his life up to that point. He thought about the many girlfriends he'd had in high school. The one-nighters he'd bragged about to his friends. The casual encounters. He thought about college. Those first few months where he felt like he ruled the world. He thought about Benton Sage and his honest words. His suggestion that Cabot change his ways before he screwed everything up. He remembered packing up Benton's things. Reading Benton's journal. Finding the notes in the margins at the school library. He pulled into a grocery store parking lot and killed the engine. He walked inside. He scanned the large room for anyone who looked useful to him. Walking around the checkout lanes, Cabot grabbed a pack of gum, tossed it down onto the nearest cashier's conveyer belt, and tapped his fingers on the counter. On his way out, he stopped and turned to a tall bag boy with closely cut hair and asked him his name.

"Neil," he said.

"Okay, Neil. Here's the thing. You know a guy named Cullen?" Cabot asked.

"Yeah. Cullen Witter."

"Yeah? Friend of yours?"

"Went to school with me. He's a year younger, though," Neil said.

"Oh," Cabot replied, "I need to talk to him."

"So what?"

"Well, Neil, would ten bucks get me his address?" Cabot asked, taking out his wallet.

"I guess. I think he lives over off Eighth Street on the gravel road," Neil said nonchalantly.

"Eighth Street?" Cabot said in that I-don't-know-my-way-around-here manner.

"Right," Neil said back.

"Neil, you've been a tremendous help," Cabot said, smacking the ten into Neil's hand.

Cabot walked toward his car and, after passing two people up, stopped the third and asked, with a face full of confusion and innocence, how to find Eighth Street.

"Okay," the woman began, "keep goin' down Main Street till you get to Machen Drive, then take a right and as soon as you pass the four-way stop, you're there."

"Is that a paved road?" Cabot asked.

"Yeah," the woman answered.

"Thanks."

In his motel room, Cabot could hear the sound of clanks, bangs, and heavy motors outside as a crew tore down the motel's existing sign to replace it with the new one. He tried taking a nap, but the noise proved too distracting. He watched a few minutes of television before getting a headache and deciding against that idea as well. He had picked up a *Lily Press* from the grocery store on his way out, so he sat at the room's small desk, flipped on the lamp, and began to read through it. The cover story was about the Lazarus woodpecker. Of course, Cabot could barely read the name Lazarus without thinking about his Bible. He remembered the story of Lazarus being told to him in Sunday school. He remembered wondering what it would have been like to witness Jesus roll the stone away from Lazarus's tomb and watch the dead man walk out, still wearing his grave clothes. The article was about several of the town's businesses embracing the recent tourism boom brought to Lily by the sighting of the bird. Cabot laughed when he read about the Lazarus Burger and laughed even louder when the article mentioned some woman giving woodpecker haircuts. But still, all Cabot could really think about was Alma, and more specifically, what he would like to do to the little punk she would be going out with that night. Over those several hours he tried talking himself into just flying home and being done with the whole thing, but he knew he couldn't just let his long trip be wasted. So he packed his things, locked the door to the motel room, and drove off down the street. He followed the directions given to him and was soon putting on his turn signal at the gravel road.

Gabriel Witter laughed as Cullen ran childishly down the hallway toward his bedroom, having just shouted the strangest combination of words he'd ever heard. He repeated them back to himself. "Ornithological cannibalism," he said, as he turned off his television and opened up a small green notebook filled with page after page of song lyrics. He turned to the first blank page and, after reaching up to grab a pen off his desk, drew a picture of a woodpecker eating a hamburger. He grinned when he was done and heard a car pull up and a door slam shut. Looking out the window, he saw Lucas's car speeding away, dust floating everywhere. He looked over to the side yard to see that his dad's work truck was gone, and as he walked down the hall toward the kitchen he noticed that his mom was asleep on the living room couch. He quietly poured Fruity Pebbles into a shiny white bowl and then opened the refrigerator with an I-hope-this-doesn't-make-a-loud-sound expression on his face. After grabbing the milk, which was nearly empty, he shut the refrigerator door with the same stealth by which he'd opened it. He emptied out the jug onto his cereal and sat down to eat. Gabriel read over the newspaper his dad had left sitting there that morning, shaking his head at the long article about the bird and turning immediately to the classified ads. He was in the market for a set of drums. There were none listed in the paper. At the sink, he washed the remaining cereal out of his bowl, taking special care to make sure no colorful residue remained on the white edges and nearly burning his hands with hot water while doing so. He dried his hands off and grabbed the empty milk jug off the counter. Several previously discarded items fell to the floor when he opened the trash can. He picked them up, took the lid off the can, and painstakingly pulled the bag out while trying not to make very much noise. After finally getting the milk jug down into the bag, he tied the bright yellow plastic strings and quietly opened the back door. Gabriel tossed the bag into the large green trash can resting against the right side of the house, then yanked it into rolling position and made his way with it down the long, rocky driveway.

Cabot made his way down the gravel road slowly, and after passing two houses on the right, realized that he'd forgotten to ask the grocery store kid which house belonged to Cullen Witter. He continued on, though, hoping he'd see some name posted up on a mailbox or near a front door. As he rounded a curve, he saw what looked to be a teenager pulling a large green trash can toward the street. He pulled slightly into the driveway and waited for the boy, who wore a faded black T-shirt, to come closer. As he approached, the boy squinted and raised his free hand to block out the setting sun's glow. He set the trash can down on its base and began to speak.

"Looking for someone?" he said politely.

"Witter?" Cabot managed to spit out nervously.

"Yeah?" the boy answered, looking around at his house.

"Umm . . . can you help me with something?" Cabot asked, struggling to come up with a game plan.

"Sure," Gabriel answered, walking over to the driver's side window.

"That's all right," Cabot said, opening the door and stepping out.

"You lost or something?" the boy asked.

"I guess. I dunno. Maybe," Cabot said, looking back into the car behind him.

"Well, do you need to use the phone?"

Cabot quickly reached into the window of the car and into the backseat, where he grabbed a metal flashlight holding four D-cell batteries. He brought it up to his chest and stood before the boy, sweat dripping from his anxious forehead. The boy, still squinting in the sunlight, looked at the flashlight with confusion, and just as he went to look down the street in the direction the man had come from, Cabot lunged forward, swinging the metal and glass, knocking the boy square in the side of his head. The boy fell to the ground. Cabot immediately looked all around him. The neighborhood seemed quieter and emptier than any place he'd ever been in his entire life. The boy did not move. Cabot tossed the flashlight back into the car, walked around to the back, and opened the trunk. He picked up the boy, straining to lift him up high enough to get him into the trunk, and dropped him in as gently as possible. He looked down at the unconscious boy and whispered, "Your date's been canceled, Cullen Witter." He closed the trunk, got into the car, and drove slowly back toward town.

He sat in the parking lot of a small convenience store near the interstate for a few minutes, frantically trying to come up with a next step. He looked nervously in his rearview mirror but saw nothing more than cars passing idly by and the darkened interior of the store. He listened intently, waiting for the boy to stir or begin screaming for help. But nothing happened. He heard not a sound. Only his own shaky breathing. His own anxious heart. He decided, after considering his options, that knocking him out cold would not be enough to scare Cullen Witter into leaving Alma Ember alone. What he needed to do, he thought, was really make an impact. Really show this kid the seriousness of the situation he'd gotten himself into. With that, Cabot Searcy turned onto the interstate and made his way to Little Rock, his radio turned up, his fingers snapping, his lips moving.

When he came to, Gabriel Witter found himself in complete darkness. He tried to sit up but only smashed his head into something metal and hard. All around him was the sound of movement, and grabbing the side of his head, he thought he heard music faintly coming from somewhere nearby. It took him a few minutes to adjust to the darkness, and as his eyes fixed on the red glow of the corners of his cage, he realized just where he was. In that brief moment, Gabriel thought about how being stuffed in a trunk never really happened in real life and how it was so much different than he'd always imagined during childhood games of cops and robbers. He thought about calling out but knew that this would only cause more trouble. He remembered the man standing in front of him. Charging him. Swinging at him. He was completely confused about why it had all happened, but he wasn't naive enough for one moment to start cooking up any clever plans for escaping. His body drenched in sweat, Gabriel tried his best not to move, hoping this would relieve the aching of his head.

The movement stopped then, and he heard the metallic creak

of the car door opening. The footsteps were almost loud enough to count, as if they were being echoed from all around him. When light suddenly burst into the car, Gabriel sprang up as one would do in the middle of a nightmare. He peered up to see his captor standing over him, a concrete ceiling and walls behind him, fluorescent lights on either side.

"Can you stand?" the man asked, pulling Gabriel from the trunk.

"Yeah, I think so," Gabriel said, now leaning one side against the car.

"You probably already guessed who I am," the man said.

"I have no idea," Gabriel said, rubbing the side of his head.

"You know Alma, right?"

"Ember?" Gabriel asked, looking around at the vacant parking garage.

"Searcy. Her last name's Searcy," Cabot said sternly.

"Oh. We used to go to church together. She was Ember the last time I saw her."

"You must think I'm some dumb-ass or something, huh?" Cabot raised his voice slightly.

"I don't know anything about you except that you have a pretty big flashlight," Gabriel answered.

"Cullen, this is not your lucky day."

"Cullen?" Gabriel asked.

"Yeah, I know who you are," Cabot said, nearly smiling.

"I'm Gabriel. Gabriel Witter."

"Cut the shit, kid."

"No. Really."

"Really?" Cabot asked, his face red.

"Cullen's my older brother."

"Shit," Cabot said.

"I'm so confused," Gabriel said.

"Shit. Shit. Shit."

"Are you gonna take me back home now?"

"Shit. Shit. Shit. I can't believe this. I can't believe this." Cabot shook his head.

"Look, you obviously have some serious stuff to deal with, so if you wanna just take me home, we'll forget about the whole thing. Deal?" Gabriel asked.

"Shit. I'm a damn kidnapper now. How old are you?"

"Fifteen. But let me go. It doesn't matter. Just let me go."

"And then you'll tell someone and all of a sudden I'll be all over the news and they'll come find me somewhere and cuff me and take me to jail. Oh Jesus. I can't believe this."

"Look, I don't even know your name, okay? So, why don't you just get in your car, drive away, and we'll be done with it?" Gabriel pleaded.

"That's too easy. There's some trick. You're gonna give me up. I would. I mean, who wouldn't want the guy who knocked him out and stuffed him in a trunk to go to jail? That's crazy! Shit."

"Get in the car and drive away," Gabriel said, trying to sound forceful.

"I'm gonna need you to get back in the trunk now," Cabot said with surprising calmness.

"No."

"Do it now," Cabot said, stepping forward.

"Just let me go home. It's so easy. Just let me go."

"I can't. Get in." Cabot held up the same flashlight he'd used earlier, and his face went a particular shade of angry that Gabriel wasn't sure he'd ever seen on anyone in his life. Already dizzy from the first hit and knowing that he'd probably end up falling down flat on his face if he made a run for it, Gabriel followed Cabot's orders.

As he closed the trunk door on Gabriel for the second time, Cabot noticed the picture on his shirt. It was a white figure, a man, with long wings behind him. He was stretching one arm out up above his head, toward the sky. Sitting back down in the driver's seat, Cabot gripped the steering wheel and placed his forehead down against it. He thought about taking the boy up on his offer, figuring that maybe he was telling the truth. Maybe he wouldn't tell anyone. And if he did, maybe he really didn't know his name. But he knew the boy would put it all together. He'd figure it all out. It would be no time at all until Cabot wasn't changing the world, but sitting alone in a jail cell with a bologna sandwich and a lidless toilet. He couldn't let that happen. He started the car. He thought about the boy's shirt. The white figure with wings. He thought about the boy's name. Gabriel, the Left Hand of God. Pulling out of the parking garage, Cabot Searcy began to piece together the drawn-out puzzle that the last four years of his life had been. Benton's suicide, the Book of Enoch, the Watchers, the vision of God, Gabriel, and the bird. The hours spent studying the fallen angels, the Grigori. The time spent theorizing and debating over the fact that God himself had stifled the greatness of human potential.

Everything that had, in some way or another, led him to some nothing town where, as it seemed, things could come back from the dead, mistakes could be rectified, lives could be started over. And as he stopped at a red light just around the corner, Cabot Searcy realized his destiny.

CHAPTER NINETEEN
A Lavish Journey

🐾   I decided that Lucas Cader was my hero for punching John Barling in the eye, even if it had turned out that he was just some sad guy looking for fame and fortune. He'd still brought all this shit into town that I felt was unnecessary, and I wouldn't soon forget it. And judging by his battle wound, I didn't think Lucas would either. Mena told me one night after it happened that Lucas had to be pulled off the stage and was quite lucky that he didn't get charges pressed against him. I couldn't believe it. I mean, Lucas Cader beating up some bird guy. It was nearly as crazy as there being a bird guy in town in the first place.

"Your shirt's cool," Mena said to me as we three made our way into Burke's one afternoon.

"It's Gabriel's. I've been raiding his closet," I said.

"Oh. I knew you weren't that cool," Mena joked, punching me in the arm.

"Cooler than your banged-up boyfriend," I joked back.

"Hey, ass-hat, what the hell?" Lucas said, slapping my arm with the back of one hand.

"Don't start beating me up, Captain Ahab, I'm just joking," I said, laughing.

For some reason, Mr. Burke, who, of course, owned Burke's Burger Box, thought that because my brother had gone missing he could help me out by giving me free hamburgers. So, and this was only the second time, he walked over to our table, leaned down, and whispered to us that he'd take care of the bill. We thanked him, asked no questions, and I rolled my eyes to Lucas and Mena as he walked away. What I noticed that summer was that people generally have no idea how to react to strange situations like the one my family had been put into. People just couldn't quite seem to figure out how to help or what to say or what not to say, even. They tried giving us things and offering us advice and putting different kinds of books in our mailbox. And then there were the avoiders. These were the people who bothered me most. These were the ones who, as soon as we walked in somewhere, tried their best not to make eye contact, or hid behind a food aisle, or pretended they didn't see us altogether. I just couldn't understand how these people justified avoiding not just me but my entire family. My mom said that people didn't like being put in the uncomfortable position of speaking to us. I said that was bullshit.

People didn't like having to come up with something smart or helpful or sensitive to say, and they weren't intelligent enough to realize that all we wanted, all *I* wanted, was to be treated the same as I had been three months before. I wanted to be ignored because of my eccentricities, not because of my brother. And I wanted to be offered help from people because they cared about me, not because they felt some strange social obligation to do so. I wanted the world to sit back, listen up, and let me explain to it that when someone is sad and hopeless, the last thing they need to feel is that they are the only ones in the world with that feeling. So, if you feel sorry for someone, don't pretend to be happy. Don't pretend to care only about their problems. People aren't stupid. Not all of us, anyway. If someone's little brother disappears, don't give him a free hamburger to make him feel better—it doesn't work. It's a good burger, sure, but it means nothing. It means something only to the Mr. Burkes of the world. But people will do these things. They did them all summer long. Offering free meals, free stays in condos in Florida, even free plumbing. And we let them. We let them because *they* needed it, not us. We didn't let them help us because we needed it, we let them help us because inside of humans is this thing, this unnamed need to feel as if we are useful in the world. To feel as if we have something significant to contribute. So, old ladies, make your casseroles and set them on doorsteps. And old men, grill your burgers and give them to teenagers with cynical worldviews. The world can't be satisfied, but that need to fix it all can.

Book Title #87: *Alone in the World with This Feeling.*

Dr. Webb says that had Lucas Cader never met my family, he may very well have slipped into the same messed-up life that had ended both his father and brother. And I thought about this very thing one night as Lucas and I played basketball in the dark outside my garage. I thought about how terrible I was at basketball and about how Lucas Cader seemed quite used to ignoring that and continued playing with me.

"I've decided that I'll probably marry Mena," he said, going for a free throw.

"Yeah?" I asked.

"Seems to fit well, don't you think?"

"Actually, yeah. I do," I said back, retrieving the ball from the grass.

"And you, Cullen, you'll be the best man, of course." He laughed.

"Well, of course," I said.

"And when we have kids, well, you know who'll be the god-father," Lucas said, dribbling the ball.

"Well, could it be Cullen Witter?" I said, pointing to myself.

"Nah, Gabriel's more responsible than you. But I'm sure he'll let you help," Lucas said, throwing the ball.

I stood there silent. With such confidence and no awkward-ness at all, Lucas had mentioned my brother as if he were merely inside the house listening to music or watching TV or writing down song lyrics. I sat down on the ground. I rested myself back on both hands, looking up toward the sky. And even though there were no visible stars, I smiled. I smiled and I pictured my brother holding some baby in his arms. Singing some childish song. Dancing some silly dance.

The next morning, feeling slightly guilty about having kicked Lucas out of our house and thereby causing him to assault an ornithologist to prove his allegiance to my family, I suggested that we go down to the White River and take one of Merle's Famous Lazarus Boat Tours.

"You're kidding?" Lucas asked, looking up from his cereal.

"I'm not. Come on, it'll be fun," I said, leaning over to slip on my shoes.

"Is this some sort of trick? Are you going to dump my body into the river, Cullen?" he joked.

"Yes. But not today. Today we join expert tour guide Merle Hodge on a lavish journey through the Arkansas bayous to seek out the elusive Lazarus woodpecker." I raised my hands dramatically into the air as I spoke.

"Well, it will be interesting to see what a fisherman suddenly knows about a woodpecker that no one's even seen in sixty years," Lucas replied.

"Won't it?" I jumped up from my seat and headed for the door.

Here's why Merle Hodge was now the proprietor and sole employee of Merle's Famous Lazarus Boat Tours: He was the previous proprietor and sole employee of Merle's Famous Fisherman Tours. That is, until the U.S. Fish and Wildlife Service declared the entire area around Lily to be part of the Cache River National Wildlife Refuge. By doing this, hunters and fishermen all around had lost the land and water they'd stalked and camped on and thrown bait into for most of their lifetimes. This caused perhaps the most publicized dissent against the Lazarus woodpecker, with op-ed pieces running weekly in the paper to disparage John Barling and his mob of birdwatcher friends. There were even rumors of secret meetings of a group called Bird Haters United. I had thought seriously of attending one of their meetings.

It turns out that a deluxe, all-inclusive tour through the Cache River National Wildlife Refuge costs twenty-five dollars per person and lasts roughly three hours. Each in our own kayaks, complete with camouflage life vests and double-ended paddles, we headed out.

When one is an hour and fifteen minutes into a three-hour boat tour and realizes that he knows just as much about the area as his tour guide, if not more, he begins to stare down into the clear, cold water and focuses his attention on the way the midday sun is reflecting off the river bottom. Then, as he overhears Merle Hodge say some nonsense about the Lazarus woodpecker and make four or five grammatical mistakes, he imagines Gabriel Witter floating casually up beside him, tapping his paddle against his older brother's kayak, and giving him a don't-make-fun-of-this-poor-guy look. Then, just as he reaches over to pull his younger brother closer to him, to see if he's real, he pictures a dark shadow covering them entirely. He looks up to see, there in the sky and blocking out the sun completely, the long-lost Lazarus woodpecker, with its wings outspread and its beak pointing upward, nearly piercing the blue of the sky. He looks back down to find that his brother is no longer there. He is no longer there to stop him from ridiculing Merle Hodge or making some smart-ass remark about woodpeckers. He doesn't stop him when he thinks about asking the tour guide an unanswerable question or when he considers pretending to see a large bird off in the distance. He isn't there anymore to supply Cullen Witter with endless chances to do better.

"Do you think they'll ever find him?" I asked Lucas as we drove home that evening.

"I know they will," Lucas said confidently.

"And you're serious when you say that? I mean, you actually *believe* that, don't you?"

"I really do, Cullen," Lucas said bluntly, his gaze on the road ahead.

Book Title #88: *Some Childish Song*.

CHAPTER TWENTY
The Boy Who Caused Silence

🜇   Some two weeks after being stuffed into a trunk, Gabriel Witter sat on the edge of a mostly comfortable bed with a brown and orange quilt draped over his shoulders. He hummed some songs he'd heard before being abducted and thought briefly about whether or not he really was the reincarnation of the archangel Gabriel, which is exactly what Cabot Searcy had told him was the truth. He was amused at the thought of being anything but an overly curious teenager. As the door across the empty room opened, he stood up with a look of excitement.

"Sit back down," Cabot Searcy told him, blocking the doorway.

About once a day since they'd arrived wherever they were, Cabot would come into Gabriel's small, windowless room, sit in a wooden chair across from him, look at him with anxiety and hesitation in his eyes, and ask him strange questions like, "What's heaven like?" and "Am I doing everything right?" Gabriel would rarely give answers to these questions, usually staring blankly back at his captor or asking politely to be freed. Cabot Searcy never got close enough to touch Gabriel. He never brought anything into the room like a flashlight or a gun. He only came in quietly, sat down, and began sharing his wild ideas.

Three weeks into his stay, Gabriel asked Cabot Searcy where they were. Cabot stood up, pushed the chair back against the wall where he'd gotten it, turned around to walk out, and said plainly, "We're in a room." Gabriel was not the type of boy to assume that he had to merely yell or bang on walls or jump up and down against the floor to get someone's attention from the outside. He was not so dumb as to believe that rescue was an easy task. Instead he sat there quietly. He thought about his friends. Libby Truett, the girl he loved. Lucas Cader, the only person who could beat him at Monopoly. He pictured his mom crying at the hair salon, slowly wrapping an old woman's hair around curlers. He saw his dad putting up posters with some dorky school picture of himself on the front and a meager reward offered underneath. And when he thought about Cullen, he began to get upset for the first time since he'd been there. He knew how his brother was. Always thinking about every little thing. Always taking one sentence that someone had said and dissecting it until it meant nothing. He knew his brother would be in his room, not going through his things, but studying them. He knew he would feel hopeless. Alone. He knew Cullen Witter would blame himself without even really knowing what had happened.

"It's been five weeks," Gabriel said as Cabot Searcy handed him a paper plate with a ham and cheese sandwich on it.

"And one day," Cabot said back, sitting down in the chair.

"So," Gabriel began, taking a bite of the sandwich, "if I am an angel, what's stopping me from just flying out of here?"

"It doesn't work like that, I guess," Cabot said.

"Well, that doesn't make sense. I mean, if I had all these powers, I'm sure I'd be using them for something. At least to get a TV in here."

The next day Cabot Searcy toted in a small black and silver television, set it down on the floor in the far corner of the room, plugged it in, and said, "There," before walking back out and locking the door from the outside. Gabriel nearly threw himself onto the floor and, scooting across the room to the TV, thought he might start crying. He pushed the power button and was met with a screen full of white and black squiggly lines. He tried turning a channel. Nothing happened. He looked around to the back of the TV to find that it was merely plugged into the wall. No cable. No channels. He left it on, though, turning the volume up as loud as it would go, and he sat there, in the middle of the floor, letting the sound of a million bugs flying around him, of planes taking off, of cars colliding, of paper being balled up, of driving through a tunnel, fill the room. He held one ear closed with one hand and, letting it go, held the other. He did this for a while, making different noises out of the cacophony surrounding him. Cabot Searcy walked into the room, turned the TV off, and looked down at Gabriel on the floor.

"What the hell?" he said.

"There's no cable," Gabriel said, never getting up.

"I'm working on it, okay?" Cabot said, storming back out and slamming the door.

"He's working on it," Gabriel whispered to himself, lying all the way down on his back and staring at the ceiling to see the all-too-familiar rough whiteness sprinkled with the tiniest flecks of gold sparkle.

Six weeks and four days after being mistaken for his brother, Gabriel lay in bed, flipping through the channels of the television. Cabot Searcy had, in all his brilliance, run a long black cable under the door from whatever room was outside and hooked it to the back of the TV. After doing this, he had taken a towel or something and shoved it under the crack in the door. Gabriel Witter, unable to sleep in complete darkness, had finally started to get rest since the television arrived. He stopped on a news station and waited for himself to be mentioned. Just as he'd noticed the week before, he was nowhere to be found. He did, however, figure out that he was somewhere in Georgia, having accidentally stumbled onto a local Atlanta news station. He knew that he couldn't be sure whether he was in the city or somewhere outside of it. He had thought for hours about ways to escape, from pretending to be violently ill to hiding behind the door with the television and throwing it onto Cabot's head. He knew, though, that nothing would work out the way it did in movies. He wouldn't make it across the street or to a neighbor's house. He wouldn't have the heart to hurt Cabot enough to get that far. And he knew that Cabot would come back, and the next time, it might be for Cullen instead.

Cabot Searcy walked into the room on the day that marked week ten and took his regular seat. He smiled at Gabriel, who was just waking up, and stared at him as if waiting to hear something important.

"What?" Gabriel said, wiping his eyes.

"You'd tell me if this was all a test, right?" Cabot asked him.

"If what was all a test?"

"If me taking you and keeping you here and finding all the books and stuff. If it's all some test from God. Well, you'd tell me. Wouldn't you?"

"Okay. I'm gonna say this one last time. *I am just a kid*," he said slowly, as if talking to an elderly person or a small child.

"Rii-ii-ight." Cabot nodded.

"Fine. I'm Gabriel. I'm God's right-hand man," Gabriel said.

"Left hand, you mean," Cabot corrected.

"Whatever. Sure. What happens now?" Gabriel asked.

"Well, I've been thinking about that a lot," Cabot said.

"And?"

"And it seems to me that in order to get things back the way they're supposed to be, you have to go," Cabot said with some hesitation.

"Go home, you mean?" Gabriel asked.

219

"Not exactly. Home as in heaven. To be with God. Do you get my drift?" Cabot asked.

"Okay," Gabriel said, staring at the floor, "let's recap, if that's all right."

"Sure."

"You went to college and your roommate killed himself on Christmas Day."

"Right."

"And you found a verse in his journal that led you to an ancient Bible in the school's library."

"Enoch, right."

"And from there you read this guy's notes, read the book, and determined that had Gabriel—"

"You!" Cabot butted in.

"Had *I* not followed God's orders to stop these fallen angels from living with the humans, then people, us, everyone, would have been taught to be as smart and powerful as God himself?"

"Bingo," Cabot said.

"So, you really think that these angels were that smart?"

"Smart, but misunderstood. They wanted to help us down here. And you stopped them from doing that."

"But it's what God told me to do," Gabriel said, playing along.

"But God has now told *me* to do *this*. He has led me to all these things. He led me to that school and to Benton Sage and to finding the books. He led me to Savannah to marry Alma, and then he led me to Lily where I accidentally took you. Only, it wasn't an accident. That's the way it was all supposed to happen. It's amazing how it all fits, isn't it?"

Gabriel looked at Cabot Searcy and, for a moment, thought of the many things he could say to him to shatter his delusions. He thought of quoting from the Bible, but changed his mind. He thought of once again denying his heavenliness, but didn't. He wanted to call Cabot crazy. Misinformed. Confused. He wanted to scream to him that God would never lead a man to take a boy from his family. But he didn't. Instead Gabriel Witter stood up, raised both hands into the air, and began to shout as sincerely and convincingly as he could manage.

"Oh God. Do with me what you will!"

And with that Cabot Searcy got up, walked through the door, and shut it behind him. Gabriel heard banging from the other room. He heard two quick yells, as if two people were arguing or one person was arguing with himself. He leaned his ear against the door, his breathing heavy and deep, his eyes closed. He heard words like "shit" and "damn" and "help me." He heard the slamming of cabinet doors, the tapping of shoes on hard tile, the whir of a ceiling fan. Gabriel listened as Cabot Searcy yelled the following:

"I have sinned. I have sinned. Help me, oh Lord. I have sinned."

Hearing footsteps coming quickly his way, Gabriel threw himself onto the bed and didn't take his eyes off the door. It swung open, slammed into the wall, bounced back only slightly, and Cabot approached the bed. He looked down. He was breathing hard. His face was wet with what Gabriel assumed were tears. Cabot kneeled down. He took one hand and placed it on Gabriel's shoulder. Closing his eyes, he began to speak.

"Gabriel, I need you to tell me the truth. I trust that God will tell me the truth through your voice. So, tell me. Tell me what I'm supposed to do."

"I don't know what you're supposed to do," Gabriel said as calmly as possible. "Don't you see that?"

"You have to!" Cabot shot up, beginning to yell. "I can't breathe. I can't think. This should be easier. Alma and Cullen and back in Savannah. It's all connected. It has to be. It has to make sense. Benton killed himself for this! He just left! Just like that! He just gave up! It was too hard! But I figured it out, right? I did it, right? I'm the one! I'm the one to finish the job. I'm the one to make things right!"

"Where's your family?" Gabriel said, sitting up on the bed.

"What?" Cabot had tears streaming down his face.

"Your family. Where are they? Do they know who you are? Do they know how important you are?" Gabriel asked, now beginning to stand.

"Shut up! Quit distracting me!"

Cabot grabbed at the sides of his own angry face. He appeared to be trying to knock the thoughts out of his head. Gabriel stood up and, though he thought about running for the door, he fell to his knees, clasped his hands, and began to pray.

"Lord, help this man find his way without hurting himself or anyone else. Help him find his heart, Lord, the same heart that has provided me food and warmth. Help him, please. Please help him to stop and think."

"Stop it, stop it, STOP IT!" Cabot took both hands and knocked Gabriel onto his side. He kicked at Gabriel's back and legs. He sniffled, cried, and reached down to pick Gabriel up and flung him across the room. Gabriel's head smashed into the side of the television and he fell motionless and sprawled out on the hard floor.

"You should've just told me the truth," Cabot said, slowly approaching the boy.

Though his face was pressed coldly against the floor, Gabriel whispered quietly and with certainty in his voice. Cabot yelled, "What? Speak up!"

"You're not the one," Gabriel said more clearly, pain in his voice.

With that, Cabot Searcy sat down on the edge of the bed, looked down at Gabriel Witter and his bleeding scalp, and said nothing. He looked over to the television to see a shot of a news program being broadcast from Lily, Arkansas. A small caption appeared under an image of a reporter standing before a patch of swampy woods. The caption read NO SECOND CHANCES IN LILY, ARKANSAS.

Cabot began to laugh. He got louder and louder and finally stopped, abruptly, as he looked back down at the motionless figure on his floor.

"It's time to say good-bye, Gabriel," Cabot muttered, standing up and switching off the television.

CHAPTER TWENTY-ONE

The Meaning of This Is Not to Save You

When I saw John Barling tossing a large brown duffel bag into the back of his truck, I remained on my porch and tried my best to read his lips as he mumbled under his breath. I couldn't make out any words, but I imagined them to be things that one wouldn't hear in church. He slammed the back door shut and, looking up at me, gave me the quickest of salutes with his right hand before hopping into the driver's seat, starting the loud engine up, and driving off. I saw Fulton Dumas run around from the side of his house, yelling "HELL YES!" and "ALL RIGHT!" while throwing a handful of rocks toward the road. He caught a glimpse of me, waved one hand uncomfortably my way, and walked back into his house.

The Lazarus woodpecker weighs approximately twenty-six ounces, is twenty-four inches tall, and has a wing span of just around thirty-two inches. This would make it, as I mentioned once before, the largest woodpecker in existence. This would all be true if the bird existed, which it didn't. It did in the 1940s, but not in Lily, Arkansas. Not the summer my brother went missing. Not in the woods near the White River. Not in John Barling's poorly shot photograph. Not in the sightings on the highway. Not in the DNA tests done by the National Audubon Society of a feather found by a young girl and her dog.

Instead, what had my entire town full of hope and big ideas was what one scientist described on the news as an extremely rare group of albino woodpeckers by the name of pileated.

"They're big birds," the scientist told the reporter, "just not quite as big as the Lazarus was."

Aside from being completely different species, there is a significant yet odd difference in the color of the Lazarus woodpecker and the pileated one, the latter having a distinctly darker bill. Given that the bird or birds seen near my home and supposedly seen all around town were albino species, their bills were just about the color that the Lazarus's would have been. This, supported by the inability to trap or record an actual bird and the negative DNA tests, all led to the conclusion that my town had been living a lie for nearly four months. And if you listened closely outside of any window in Lily the week we found out, you could hear the deafening silence and disappointment.

"This guy at the store told me something cool today," Lucas said to me as we sat idly on the porch.

"What's that?" I asked.

"He told me the Lazarus used to be called the Good God Bird."

"Yeah? That's weird," I said.

"Native Americans," he said.

"Native Americans what?" I asked.

"They used to see it flying over their heads and in trees and the only thing they could do was yell 'GOOD GOD!' 'cause it looked so big." Lucas smirked, shaking his head slightly from side to side, his hands spread apart to signify the bird's enormousness in the air.

I wondered, riding in the passenger seat of my mom's car one afternoon, whether there would ever be a break in the silence that now seemed to occupy all of my family's time together. An awkwardness had sprung up after those few months, where before there would have been playful laughter and in-depth conversation and harmless bickering between us. I wondered if Lucas Cader would really marry Mena Prescott and if Gabriel would actually be there to hold their children. I wondered if Russell Quitman would ever walk again or if Ada Taylor had sentenced herself to a life of sitting around and waiting on him hand and foot. Then I realized that I didn't care.

Dr. Webb says that life is so full of complications and confusion that humans oftentimes find it hard to cope. This leads to people throwing themselves in front of trains and spending all their money and not speaking to their relatives and never going home for Christmas and never eating anything with chocolate in it. Life, he says, doesn't have to be so bad all the time. We don't have to be so anxious about everything. We can just be. We can get up, anticipate that the day will probably have a few good moments and a few bad ones, and then just deal with it. Take it all in and deal as best we can. We can learn to love the Mena Prescotts, we can imagine the Russell Quitmans to be zombies, we can fantasize all day long about the Ada Taylors, and we can wish we were more like the Lucas Caders. We can be comforted in the fact that life will always be a struggle. There will always be false hopes. Lazarus woodpeckers. There will be John Barlings to lead us astray and Oslo Foukes to remind us that maybe we *are* doing things right after all.

When I asked him the meaning of life, Dr. Webb got very quiet and then told me that life has no one meaning, it only has whatever meaning each of us puts on our own life. I'll tell you now that I still don't know the meaning of mine. And Lucas Cader, with all his brains and talent, doesn't know the meaning of his, either. But I'll tell you the meaning of all this. The meaning of some bird showing up and some boy disappearing and you knowing all about it. The meaning of this was not to save you, but to warn you instead. To warn you of confusion and delusion and assumption. To warn you of psychics and zombies and ghosts of your lost brother. To warn you of Ada Taylor and her sympathy and mothers who wake you up with vacuums. To warn you of two-foot-tall birds that say they can help, but never do.

When one is sitting in his bedroom and, happening to glance out the window, sees his little brother walking slowly down the driveway, he immediately jumps up, knocks over a stack of magazines piled up beside him, and runs through the doorway and down the hall. He throws open the front door, slams his body against the screen and, hearing the *tap tap tap* behind him, jumps over the porch steps and down to the driveway. He stands several yards in front of his brother. He considers running, but doesn't. His arms and legs are shaking. His bottom lip between his teeth, he walks slowly and carefully, making not a sound. He stops, reaches one arm out, and pokes Gabriel Witter on the left shoulder with his index finger. He smiles the slightest of smiles.

Book Title #89: *Where Things Come Back.*

Acknowledgments

This novel, in all of its incarnations, wouldn't have been possible without the assistance, inspiration, and support of many people.

I am endlessly and wholeheartedly grateful to Ken Wright, who took this novel under his wing and made sure to find it the perfect home; Namrata Tripathi, editor extraordinaire, who fell in love with this story and helped make it better than I ever thought it could be; and John Meils and the people at WeBook, who rescued me from literary obscurity.

There would be no story to tell had it not been for my parents, Wayne and Karen Whaley, who always let me be who I was: a loner with a knack for writing semi-depressing stories; my brother and sister, Brian and Deena, for the impact they've had on my growing up; and my extended family—from aunts and uncles to cousins and grandparents—whose lives and words have, no doubt, become many of my characters' lives and words.

I will also never forget the encouragement I received before, during, and well after writing this novel. To Randi Anderson, for her skills with a highlighter and red pen; to Kimberly Powell, Charissa Sistrunk, Nate and Anna Nelson, Melody Harlon, and

Lindsay Welsh, for their unending friendship and support; to Buddy Merritt, for his tips on life; Dr. Susan Roach, for helping me appreciate being from the South; Dr. Andrew Higgins, for advising me not to settle for ordinary life; and to Genaro Ký Lý Smith, for teaching me to be a better writer. I also owe a great deal of gratitude to the many teachers I've had the honor of working with and to all of the hundreds of students, young and old, who've listened to me tell my stories for the last five years.

This story, while completely fictional, was inspired by an odd combination of the music of Sufjan Stevens; a story heard on National Public Radio; a small Arkansas town; my own hometown of Springhill, Louisiana; and a bird that refused to go away. Many thanks are owed to the above mentioned for their roles in what has been, for the past few years now, an obsession and a second life that I never expected to live.

A READING GROUP GUIDE

*Where Things Come Back
by John Corey Whaley*

1. The Book of Enoch, Gabriel, and the Fallen Angels are themes that tie together many of the main characters in complex ways. How do you view and interpret this element of the book as it relates to specific characters' lives, to the meaning of religion, and to the intelligence and potential of humankind?

2. Cabot Searcy takes on a mission he believes was Benton's idea. Why do you think Cabot becomes so obsessed with the Book of Enoch? Was he crazy? A religious zealot? Or was he simply a misguided soul looking for his own second chance?

3. Over the course of the novel, Cullen exhibits cynicism, hope, idealism, and sometimes despair. Is he acting out the stages of grief over his missing brother, or is he simply a typical, unhappy teenager trying to figure out his life? Think of the other missing brothers and sons in the novel (Oslo, Lucas's brother, Benton Sage). What is the significance of these characters' stories? How do they relate to the themes of desperation and second chances that are explored in the story?

4. Cullen has a very deep and loving connection with his brother, Gabriel. In what ways do Cullen and Gabriel appear to be a typical pair of teenage brothers? In what ways does their relationship strike you as unique or special?

5. Lily, Arkansas, is a town where things come back—both in a positive and a negative sense. Discuss both sides of this theme and the implications for the town of Lily. Do you think that Cullen Witter will end up staying in Lily?

6. The author calls *Where Things Come Back* a book about second chances. What are some of the second chances that characters get in this novel? Specifically consider John Barling and Benton Sage, in addition to the main characters. Are they always successful? Do things always turn out as they hope?

7. What is the significance of the Lazarus woodpecker, the bird that caused such excitement in the town of Lily but which never actually existed there? How can the Lazarus be symbolically interpreted?

8. The author describes many different kinds of love in this story: parental love, fraternal love, romantic love, and love for God. What does the novel say about each?

9. Consider the somewhat secondary female cast of *Where Things Come Back*—Ada Taylor, Alma Ember, and others—and their influence on the male characters of the story.

10. Cullen and Gabriel both find comfort in music throughout the novel. What is the significance of the various lyrics quoted within Cullen's narrative, and how do they relate to the scenes in which they are used?

11. Consider the format of the novel and the movement of time: how we alternate among Cullen's, Benton's, and Cabot's stories and between first- and third-person narrators until the story lines converge at the very end. How did the author's approach to time affect your reading and comprehension of the novel? How did you anticipate that the various narrative threads would intersect or be resolved?

12. Discuss the quirks of Cullen's voice—for example, his lists, his fantasies, his third-person phrasing. How did Cullen's voice influence your view of his story? How does it help us understand his mindset as the narrator?

13. Cullen keeps a running list of titles for books that he could write in the future. Consider your own life, both important events and inconsequential moments, like Cullen does. What are some titles that would fit your personal story?

14. *Where Things Come Back* is Cullen's final title idea and becomes the title of this novel. What is the significance of this title being the final line of the book? What does it imply about what happens at the end of the novel?

LISTEN: TRAVIS COATES WAS ALIVE ONCE AND THEN HE WASN'T. NOW HE'S ALIVE AGAIN. SIMPLE AS THAT.

Turn the page to start reading NOGGIN.
Another touching, hilarious and wholly original novel
from John Corey Whaley.

ADVANCED STUDIES IN CRANIAL REANIMATION

Listen—I was alive once and then I wasn't. Simple as that. Now I'm alive again. The in-between part is still a little fuzzy, but I can tell you that, at some point or another, my head got chopped off and shoved into a freezer in Denver, Colorado.

You might have done it too. The dying part, I mean. Or the choosing-to-die part, anyway. They say we're the only species on the planet with the knowledge of our own impending doom. It's just that some of us feel that doom a lot sooner than expected. Trust me when I tell you that everything can go from fine and dandy to dark and depressing faster than you can say "acute lymphoblastic leukemia."

The old me got so sick so fast that no one really had time to do anything but talk about how sick he got and how fast he got that way. And the chemo and the radiation and the bone marrow transplants didn't do anything but make him sicker faster and with much more ferocity than before.

They say you can't die more than once. I would strongly disagree. But this isn't a story about the old me dying. No one wants to hear about how I told my parents, my best friend, Kyle, and my girlfriend, Cate, that I was choosing to give up. That's a story I don't want to tell. What I do want to tell you, though, is a story about how I suddenly found myself waking up in a hospital room with my throat sore, dry and burning, like someone had shoved an entire bag of vinegar-soaked cotton balls down it. I want to tell you about how I was moving my fingers and wiggling my toes and how the doctors and nurses standing around me were so impressed with this. I'm not sure why blinking my eyes earned a round of applause and why it mattered that I was peeing into a bag, but to these people, it was like they were witnessing a true miracle. Some of the nurses were even crying.

I want to tell you a story about how you can suddenly wake up to find yourself living a life you were never supposed to live. It could happen to you, just like it happened to me, and you could try to get back the life you think you deserve to be living. Just like I did.

They told me I couldn't talk, said it was too early to try that just yet. I didn't know why, but I listened anyway. My mom and dad walked in, and she cried big tears and he went in to touch my face, and the nurse asked him to wait, asked him to please step aside until they were sure everything was working okay.

They gave me a small white board and a marker and told me to write my name. I did. Travis Ray Coates. They asked me to write down where I live. I did. Kansas City, Missouri. They asked me to write down my school. I did. Springside High. They asked me to write down the year. I did. Then the room got suddenly quiet, and even though it was bright and clean and I could smell medicine and bleach, I knew something was wrong.

This is when they told me that they'd done it. They'd gone through with the whole cranial hibernation and reanimation thing. They'd actually gone and cut my head off. I was so sure they'd put me under and changed their minds and that I'd gone through all that paperwork for nothing. But then my mom held up a mirror, and I saw that my head was shaved nearly bald and that my neck had bandages wrapped all around it. I looked pretty rough—my lips were purple and cracked, my cheeks were flushed, and my eyes were big and glazed over. Drugged, my eyes were drugged.

I'm going to tell you the truth here and say that I never, not once, not even for a tiny second, thought this crazy shit would work. And I never thought they did either. My parents, I mean. But I looked up at their wet eyes and felt their hands on my hands, and I knew right then that they were as happy as any two people had ever been. Their dead son lying on a bed in front of them, silent but with a beat in his chest again. Mary Shelley's nightmare come true, right there in a hospital in Denver.

Hospitals. I knew hospitals. I knew them like most kids know their own homes, know their neighborhoods, and know which yards to avoid and which ones it's safe to leave your bike in. I knew a nurse was only allowed to give you extra pain meds if a doctor had signed off on it first but that getting extra Jell-O only took a few smiles and maybe a joke or two, maybe a flash of the dimples. And like a factory, a hospital has its own rhythm, sounds from every room that collide in the air and echo down into your ears and repeat themselves, even in the night-time, when the world wants so bad to appear silent and quiet and peaceful. Beeps, footsteps, the tearing of plastic, spinning wheels on carts, *Wheel of Fortune* on the neighbor's TV. These were the sounds I died to, and these were the ones that welcomed me back. A world so noisy you have to lean up a bit to hear the familiar doctor as he tries to speak over it all, and just as you were starting to get used to the light, you have to close your eyes to hear him. A world that looks almost exactly the same as the one you closed your eyes to before, so much the same that you think about laughing because you got so close to being done with it all. Until you finally hear the doctor as he speaks a little louder this time.

"Welcome back, Travis Coates."

WELCOME BACK, TRAVIS COATES

When Dr. Lloyd Saranson from the Saranson Center for Life Preservation showed up at my house, I was puking in the guest bathroom with my dad sitting on the edge of the tub and patting my back. By that point I'd been sick for almost a year, seen every cancer specialist in the tri-state area, and given up all hope of survival.

Then this guy walks in and insists on pulling me out of my deathbed long enough to pitch us the craziest shit in history. And we listened because that's what desperate people do. They listen to anything you have to say to them.

"Travis," he said. "I want to save your life."

"Back of the line, buddy. No cutting." I looked to my parents with a grin, but they were either too tired or too sad to laugh.

"And how do you plan to do this?" Dad asked.

"Are you familiar with cryogenics?" Dr. Saranson asked with a serious tone.

"All right. Thanks for stopping by," Mom said, standing up and signaling for the door.

"Mrs. Coates, I wish you'd just hear me out for a few minutes. Please."

"Doctor, we've really been through a lot and—"

"Mom," I interrupted her. "Please don't take this away from me."

"Fine, go on," she said, sitting back down.

"Travis," he said. "Your body is done on this earth. We all know that. It's a sad state of affairs, but there's just no way we can change that."

"Try harder, doc. You're losing us here," I said.

"Right. That's to say, with what I'm proposing to you, that all doesn't matter anymore."

"Why's that?" I asked, looking to my parents, who were on the verge of launching from their seats and attacking him.

"Well, because in the future there'll be different ways for you to . . . exist."

"The future," I said. This wasn't something I'd given too much thought lately.

"Exactly. The future. Imagine, Travis, that you could simply fall asleep in this life and wake up in a new one someday."

"How far into the future?" I asked. In my mind I was

seeing my spaceship folding down into a suitcase like George Jetson's.

"With our latest breakthroughs we're hoping to develop the means to reanimate our first patients within a decade or two."

"You're serious, aren't you?" Dad asked.

"Quite serious, Mr. Coates."

"Has anyone else volunteered for this?" I asked.

"You'd be our seventeenth patient."

"So cryogenics," Dad said. "You want to freeze Travis with the hope of bringing him back someday?"

"Not exactly," he said. "As I was saying, Travis's body is done on this earth."

"Oh my God," Mom said quietly, this look of terror and disgust washing over her face.

"My head?" I pointed to it when I spoke, like the surgeon needed that. "You want to freeze *just* my *head*?"

"It's the only part of you not riddled with cancer cells."

This guy, he talked like he'd been there with us the whole time—with this familiarity and casualness that most strangers never used around "the dying kid." I liked it a lot, actually.

"So you knock me out and freeze my head, and I'm supposed to wake up in the future without a body and just roll with it?"

"Actually, there are several options for your hypothetical future recovery scenario, should we proceed any further."

*Options for My Hypothetical Future Recovery
Scenario (Abridged)*
1) Full-body regeneration through stem
   cell implantation into controlled
   fluid environment
2) Transplantation of full cranial
   structure onto robotic apparatus
3) Transplantation of full cranial
   structure onto donor body
4) Neuro-uploading into donor body
   and brain

*Personal Reactions to Options for My
Hypothetical Future Recovery Scenario
(Abridged)*
1) Gross
2) ROBOT ARMS!!!
3) Well, that's not happening
4) Say whaaaat?

After Dr. Saranson left that day, Mom and Dad started
laughing, which would've been really nice for a change
had I not secretly decided that I was going to volunteer
whether they liked it or not. I was tired of dying, and I
figured since this was the best idea I'd heard in months,
and didn't involve radiation or weeks of vomiting, then
I may as well go for it. I saw it like this: I was going to
die either way. Why shouldn't I be able to just fall asleep

with this slight (okay—completely impossible but still slight) possibility of my return instead of continuing on this never-ending torture fest of having everyone I love watch me slowly fade away? Maybe I'd never really get to come back, but damn it, once that idea got into my skull, there was no letting it go.

My parents took a little less convincing than I'd thought. They loved me. I was dying. This was a way for me to not be dying anymore. It was weird how simple it all became once the decision was made. I never thought knowing my actual expiration date would make a difference, but it did. It made a difference to us all. The few people who got to know we were doing it had a hard time understanding why, but in the end I think maybe they all needed the relief of letting go just as much as I did. So I let go. We let go. And then I came back. Holy shit, I came back.

It was good being back for just about as long as it took for my parents and Dr. Saranson to explain that I was attached to someone else's body. Then they had to go ahead and sedate me again because I kept clawing at my neck and ripping out my IV. The next time I woke up, my wrists and ankles had been restrained with cushiony little straps, and the looks on my parents' faces had worn a bit, like they'd forgotten how to sleep. These looks were much closer to the way I'd remembered them.

After a few days passed, and by the time I was finally allowed to speak, I was ready to have things explained more thoroughly and able to promise them that I wouldn't freak out and try to separate myself from my new body. You know, just your everyday sort of situation.

"The good news, Travis, is that you're back," Dr. Saranson began. "You're completely healthy, and now you'll get to live your life the way you were supposed to."

"And the bad news?" My voice was scratchy, raspy even.

"It isn't bad news, so much as it's a little strange and will take some getting used to."

"The body, you mean?"

"Yes. *Your* body, Travis. It belongs to you now."

"Where'd it come from?"

"A donor. A sixteen-year-old young man, like yourself, who we couldn't quite save."

"What happened to him?"

"Brain tumor," Dad said quietly.

"He knew this would happen. He wanted to save someone else's life, and that's why you're here."

"His family? Do they know about me?"

"They do. It's up to them to make contact. You know, if that's something they might want in the future. Nice people. Didn't want what Jeremy did to be a secret. They were proud of him."

"But you'll decide if you ever want to meet them or not," Dad added.

"Jeremy?" I asked.

"Yes. Jeremy Pratt," Dr. Saranson said. "Good kid."

"How long was I gone?"

"Five years last month," Mom said.

"Five years?" I asked, stunned.

"Science moved a lot faster than we could've predicted," Dr. Saranson said with a smile.

"Well, I knew you guys couldn't have aged *that* well over twenty years or something," I joked.

"Hey now," Dad said. "Don't be so sure about that."

"Are . . . are there others?" I asked.

"There's one other. A man named Lawrence Ramsey from Cleveland. We brought him back six months ago, and he is already enjoying his life again."

"He was in a Ford truck commercial last week," Dad said, rolling his eyes.

"And you know, Travis, there's probably going to be a point when you'll need someone to talk to—someone who knows a little bit about what you're going through. I'd say Lawrence would be up for that when you're ready."

"Okay. I'm not sure I'm ready for anything right now, though."

"Right. Of course. Your situation is a unique one, and it's possible and very likely that things are going to be pretty weird for a while. But you'll go back home and go back to life as normal."

"The way it was before you got sick," Mom said.

"Yes. You'll get back home, you'll go to school, you'll

make new friends. It won't be the easiest thing in the world, but you'll prove it can be done, right?"

That's when it hit me that Cate and Kyle wouldn't be Cate and Kyle anymore. They'd be these older versions of themselves that I'd have to learn about and get used to. They'd have forgotten things about me by now, especially things about the healthy version of me. They watched me die and then kept on living. I wondered if they had it in them to try again.

And *new* friends? I didn't want *new* friends. I had plenty of friends. I had a girlfriend. I had a best friend. Cate Conroy was probably sitting by the phone at her house on Twelve Oaks Road waiting to hear if I was okay or not, and Kyle Hagler was most likely on his way to her house so they could drive to the airport and get to me as soon as possible.

But they wouldn't let me just call her. I kept asking when I could call her, when I'd be able to see her, when she'd be there, and my parents just kept looking at each other like they were in a contest to see which one could go the longest without being helpful. Then Mom finally tells me some bullshit about how Cate probably needs more time to "process" all that's going on. Time to process? I mean, I was the one with the stranger's legs and arms and, let me remind you, private parts. I figured if I could process things so quickly, then why couldn't she?

"Can I just call her? I know she's waiting for me to call her."

"Travis," Mom whispered, "I have to tell you something."

"Okay."

"It's Cate, Travis." She was speaking in this calm, almost weak voice, like she was on the verge of being completely speechless.

"Cate? Is there something wrong? Did something happen?"

"She's engaged." She immediately covered her face with her hands and started crying.

I wasn't quite ready for that. This new body wouldn't react the way it should have reacted. I could barely make myself do anything at all; instead I just sat there in the sad quiet of the room. I mustered just enough energy to slump down a little in the bed and let out a kind of whimper that made me sound less like a human and more like a dying animal.

Cate was engaged. My girlfriend had a boyfriend. More than that, she was going to marry someone I'd never met. Maybe he was better than I was. I bet he even had his own body. I'd told her I'd come back for her, and even though I hadn't really believed it myself, I'd thought surely she'd believed me. I'd thought she'd wait. Why hadn't she waited for me? Why couldn't it be that I came back to life and now every little piece could fall perfectly back into its place?

But neither Kyle nor Cate ever showed up. I kept expecting it, though, every single day. I couldn't figure it out. Nothing about them not being there made any sense to me. They had *just* been there. They had *just* seen me. I had *just* seen them. I had said good-bye to them and I had closed my eyes. I had opened them and nothing. No word from either of the two people I wanted to be seeing more than anyone. Were they so different now? If it was really five years into the future, could that be all it took to change them? I mean, what's the point of getting another chance at life if everything's going to be so different that I can't stand it?

Then one night after I'd begged my parents to go to the hotel and get some rest, this nurse came in and asked if I needed anything. She was kind, and you could see that in her face and hear it in her voice.

"No, thanks," I said.

"This all must be very strange for you, huh?"

"You have no idea."

"I was there, you know."

"Where?"

"Here, I mean." She sat down in the chair by the window and looked over toward me. "When you were here before."

"You can say it," I said. "Go on. You were here when they took my head off."

"Yes. You had this little smile. It was the most surprising thing. There we were, the entire staff, watching this surgery that none of us could believe was happening. And you were so young. It was different with the other ones. You were just so young that I held my breath the whole time."

"Did you think it would work? Did you really think it was even a possibility?"

"I stayed," she said, standing up. "Some of the others transferred out after that, after what we did to you."

"Why'd you stay?"

"I needed to see it," she said. "I didn't know if it would work, but I knew if it did, then I had to be here for it, if I could."

"Ta-da." I raised my new arms slowly into the air.

"I know you're sad. Confused and probably in shock. But you don't get to come back for no reason."

"Sorry?"

"You've just been handed the keys to the kingdom, Travis. Don't waste a second of it feeling sorry for yourself."

The next day I asked to see the nurse again, and they told me she'd quit a few weeks before, that she'd resigned and moved away somewhere. Then I wondered if I'd just dreamed the whole thing up. They say you can only dream about people you've seen—either in real life or on television—that we don't have the power to create new faces in our minds, but that we recycle the thousands and thousands of faces subconsciously stored in our memories. So maybe I'd seen her five years before, in that operating room, just as they'd put me under. Maybe I'd seen her and seen her kindness, and that was all my brain had needed from her. Maybe I was remembering her now to bridge the gap. Maybe the past me and present me could find a way to coexist, keys to the kingdom in hand.

Kansas City looked pretty much the same overall, save for these strange electronic billboards all over and a new gigantic building downtown that looked like two side-by-side shiny metallic spaceships half submerged into the earth and slanted upward.

"Kaufman Center for the Performing Arts," Dad explained on our drive home from the airport. "They have concerts, plays, you know, that sort of thing."

"It looks so strange there."

"A few people got all in an uproar about it looking so modern, but they eventually settled down."

"It looks like it came from outer space."

"Yeah," he said. "It is pretty alien, I guess. But I love it. I think it's interesting."

Our house was the same in all the obvious ways, same curtains in the living room, same couch, same dining table, though it had a new centerpiece. The television was much larger and flatter than the one I remembered, no doubt something my dad had waited in a ridiculously long line for on some Thanksgiving weekend since I'd left. My first thought upon seeing it was the hope that maybe they'd put the old, still rather large TV in my bedroom.

I couldn't help noticing how walking up the stairs felt different. All the same family photos still hung on the wall, ascending up to the top. But it used to be that I couldn't see my whole face in the frames. They were just high enough so I'd see the top of my head. Now, with Jeremy Pratt's body holding me up, I was taller and I could see all the way down to the scar on my neck in every single reflection. It'd been a while since I'd taken this walk. I'd been carried up a few times after I got sick, until they decided that moving me down to the guest room made more sense, right around the time we all concluded that this thing wasn't going to go away. The hallway bathroom was terribly white and shiny clean, like it had always been, but with new towels and an automatic hand soap dispenser by the sink. I immediately stopped to use it, my parents looking on from the doorway.

"Is this a common thing now?" I asked, pulling my hand back and then placing it underneath again, and then doing that again until green soap was almost pouring over the sides, completely covering my entire palm.

"It's catching on," Mom said. "It's better for germs, I think."

"I can get behind that," I said, rinsing off my hands and wondering if this was it. Was this the furthest we'd come in five years? Where were the jetpacks? The hoverboards? If they could bring me back from the dead, why wasn't a robot greeting me at every door and asking what I needed?

Then we got to my bedroom and nothing was the same. I should say that the old TV from the living room *was* there, but nothing else looked familiar at all. There was a bed I'd never slept in, there was a dresser that hadn't held my clothes, and there was a desk where I'd never done my homework. Even the walls were different, not the green-and-white-and-maroon plaid wallpaper that had always made my friends so jealous. No, this was a light gray–colored IKEA nightmare, and I was expected to live with it.

"What happened?" I was barely able to ask.

"Travis, it's been so long," Mom said.

"Did you throw everything away?"

"It was just too hard to look at it every day. You understand?"

"We'll go shopping this week," Dad said. "We'll get you whatever you want to make it feel like home again. Okay?"

"I'm so sorry, Travis." Mom turned to walk down the hallway and into their bedroom, closing the door.

"Sorry," I said, sitting on the edge of the bed.

"This is weird for all of us," Dad said. "So weird but so amazing, too. She's just sensitive. I know you haven't forgotten that." He chuckled a bit.

"It's okay," I said. "The room, I mean. I guess I understand."

"We can make this work, huh?" he asked, looking around us at the empty, unwelcoming space.

"When did you guys know I was coming back?" I asked him.

"About two weeks before they did it," he said. "Didn't have too much time to prepare."

"She gonna be okay?"

"She'll be fine," he said. "Let's get you some dinner. You hungry?"

The kitchen smelled the same as always, like clean clothes and vanilla with just a little touch of something else—citrus, maybe—like someone was always standing around the corner peeling an orange and doing laundry.

"Eggs okay?" Dad opened the fridge.

"Sure. No cheese, though, please."

"I remember."

My dad's hair had started to gray on the sides and around his temples, but his face didn't look all that much older. He wore new glasses, black plastic frames, that looked surprisingly modern for him, I thought. I was taller than him now too, which was weird. Still is weird.

"How's work?"

"Good. You wouldn't believe how much stuff has happened since you've been away."

My dad was an executive at the largest arcade chain in the country, Arnie's Arcade, Inc. Which meant two things: 1) My dad had a job that is much cooler than all other dads' and 2) I got to hang out at the arcade all the time, even on school nights. If you've never been to Arnie's, then you're missing out. The whole idea of Arnie's is for kids to feel like they've stepped back into what Dad calls the "golden age" of video arcades. Each Arnie's looks like it's been there since before anyone inside the place was ever born. And they're full of all these classic games that can't be found in any other arcades in the country. My dad's boss, Arnold "Arnie" Tedeski, won a bunch of video game competitions back in the '80s. He was pretty famous, or so my dad tells me. Kyle and I practically lived at the Arnie's in Springside up until I got sick.

Ah, Springside. I should tell you about Springside. Springside is a neighborhood in the Country Club District of Kansas City. This district is the largest contiguous planned community in the United States, and if you're black or Jewish, you weren't allowed to live there until 1948. Also, you probably still don't live there because you're pissed off about it. Needless to say, there's a lot of snobby white people in Springside. My mom refused to send me to private school not because we couldn't afford it, but because she hated the one she'd attended as a child. It was fine, though. What my school lacked in snobbery and tacky striped ties, it more than made up for in people like Kyle and Cate. And neither of them would've ever survived in a place like Springside. But we've got shopping! Lots of shopping and parks and an Arnie's Arcade right here in Whiteside. Sorry, *Spring*side. Mostly, though, I spent my time with Kyle or Cate, and it didn't really matter what neighborhood we were in or what any of the people there thought about anything or anyone.

"Do you remember anything about being gone?" Dad slid a plate of scrambled eggs across the counter toward me.

"Not a thing. I remember closing my eyes and I remember opening them. And now this."

"Your mother used to ask me if I thought you were dreaming."

My dad started to cry as soon as he'd gotten that last sentence out. He gripped the sides of the counter with both hands and held his head down, shaking it. It looked like he was about to apologize, you know, for showing emotion, but he stopped himself and it was quiet for a while longer.

"We're so happy you're home, Travis."

"Me too."

Before bed I walked up to my parents' room and knocked on the door. My mom said to come in, and I found her lying there with puffy eyes. She'd already put on her pajamas, black ones with little red hearts all over. She sat up and smiled a little as I walked to the other side of the bed and sat down next to her.

"Well, Sharon Coates." I held an invisible microphone up in front of her. "Your only son's just come back from the dead—what do you have to say?"

#HASHTAGREADS

books worth talking about

Want to hear more from
your favourite **YA authors**?

Keen to **review** their latest titles
before anyone else?

Eager to read **exclusive extracts** and
enter **fantastic competitions**?

Join us at **HashtagReads**, home to
Simon & Schuster's best-loved
YA authors

Follow us on Twitter
@HashtagReads

Find us on Facebook
HashtagReads

Join us on Tumblr
HashtagReads.tumblr.com